"Kiss me, Anthony. Just kiss me."

He didn't get a chance to reply before Tess reached out, slipped her fingers into his hair and pulled him to her.

Anthony had known from the second he'd met her that if he let go, he'd never be able to stop kissing her.

He let go.

His mouth came down on hers hard, and she made a small sound as her lips parted, all yielding softness and insistent need. The moment ground to a stop, and the world outside fell away as if it had never existed.

All he could hear was their breaths colliding in greedy anticipation. He hadn't been the only one aching. He tasted Tess's impatience, an erotic mingling of sense and touch as her tongue swept boldly inside his mouth, another challenge, and every nerve ending in his body gathered in reply, so sharply in tune with this woman that he grabbed her to hang on.

A minute later—or a day, Anthony couldn't say—they parted. He could only stare at the sight she made with her hair ruffled around her face, her cheeks flushed and her eyes alive with pleasure and amusement.

"So, Anthony. Your blood flowing yet?"

ROMANCE

Blaze™

Dear Reader,

No matter how difficult it was for Harley and Anthony (and me!) to say goodbye in *With This Fling* (Harlequin Blaze #128), they needed to let go of their shared past to make room for the future. Harley found her *right* man, the one who will help her live and love her own happily ever after.

Now it's Anthony's turn to be the *right* man.

Tess Hardaway didn't even know she was looking for him. She knew only that life felt a bit too confining, a bit too comfortable. She wanted a challenge and, boy, did she find one. She's in for the ride of her life, because Anthony didn't think he'd get another shot at true love. But this sassy Texan has gotten under his skin, and he's hell-bent to do things right this time.

Under His Skin kicks off the new Harlequin Blaze miniseries BIG EASY BAD BOYS. Readers asked about the DiLeo family, so here they are, one story at a time—the big bad DiLeo boys in all their yummy glory. Enjoy!

Very truly yours,

Jeanie London

Books by Jeanie London

HARLEQUIN BLAZE

JEANIE LONDON
UNDER HIS SKIN

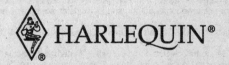

HARLEQUIN®

TORONTO • NEW YORK • LONDON
AMSTERDAM • PARIS • SYDNEY • HAMBURG
STOCKHOLM • ATHENS • TOKYO • MILAN • MADRID
PRAGUE • WARSAW • BUDAPEST • AUCKLAND

To the best sister in the world, *my* sister, Kimberly Yodzis.
You'll know why. I honestly can't imagine my life
without you, and I wouldn't want to ;-)

And special thanks to Tara Randel and her hero—*The Randy*.
Appreciated your help steering me past the flag!

ISBN 0-373-79185-2

UNDER HIS SKIN

Copyright © 2005 by Jeanie LeGendre.

www.eHarlequin.com

Printed in U.S.A.

1

"I WANT TESS HARDAWAY."

The statement came out sounding more like a demand than a request so Anthony DiLeo forced a smile at the guy behind the registration desk and tried again. "Is she around yet?"

"She was, but she left again."

"That's what you told me an hour ago."

"I know." The guy gave a lame shrug. "Sorry. You just keep missing her."

Anthony hoped like hell his bum timing didn't foreshadow the weekend ahead. Meeting Tess Hardaway was the only reason he'd come to Nostalgic Car Club's annual convention. He hadn't set eyes on her yet and already she'd given him the slip. Twice.

He tried not to look impatient. "You told me she'd be greeting people during registration."

"She has been. But she's also on the club's board—vice president of programming. She's been getting her presenters settled, too."

Okay, Tess Hardaway was a busy lady. He got that part. Anthony also got that this guy was nothing more than a volunteer. Wearing a vintage leather flying cap and goggles, he looked ready to take off in an old barnstormer. Obviously no one close to the elusive Tess Hardaway.

But he seemed to take his job seriously. He wore a T-shirt with the convention logo—a cartoon of an oversize, powerful engine plunked down in the middle of the French Quarter. The catch phrase read: Big Banger and Bourbon Street.

Anthony glanced down at the volunteer's name badge. Timmy Martin, Montgomery, Alabama.

"All right, Timmy from Montgomery. Maybe you can tell me where to find Ms. Hardaway since I'm not doing such a hot job tracking her down on my own."

"How about the AutoCarTex Foundation's hospitality suite? Have you tried there yet?"

"Didn't know AutoCarTex had a hospitality suite."

Timmy from Montgomery frowned. "Let me make a suggestion."

"Go."

"I know you wanted to register with Tess, but why don't you let me do the honors? I'll give you the registration packet and you can check out everything that's happening. Not only does AutoCarTex have a hospitality suite, but also they're hosting an event. Tess will be at both. If you want, I'll leave her a message. If she knows you're looking for her, I'm sure she'll contact you."

"Yes register. No message."

No forewarning. He couldn't risk losing the slight advantage he had in her not knowing she was being pursued. There might be a picture of her in the program. If he knew what the woman who held the titles of AutoCarTex Foundation's managing director and Nostalgic Car Club's vice president of programming looked like, he could locate his target sooner.

The guy nodded and got down to business. "Name?"

"Anthony DiLeo."

The Nostalgic Car Club apparently favored nostalgia in more than just cars. There wasn't a computer in sight, so Timmy from Montgomery searched through good old-fashioned file boxes filled with alphabetized folders.

He withdrew one and skimmed through it.

"Everything's in order, Mr. DiLeo." He offered the folder. "This has your name badge, meal tickets, driving passes, room assignment and itinerary. Let me get your bag."

Disappearing beneath the desk, he came up with a bag imprinted with the convention logo. "This has your shirt, a commemorative plaque and a booklet with all the requirements for the weekend's events. That's important if you plan to participate in any of the races. You've got paperwork to turn in."

"Got it." And Anthony did. He'd wanted Tess Hardaway and he'd gotten a convention bag instead.

He *really* hoped this wasn't an omen.

After a pit stop at the front desk, he collected his garment bag from his car and headed to his room to stow his gear.

The room was standard trendy. The hotel was standard trendy. The Chase Convention Center sat on the outskirts of Metairie, a stone's throw from New Orleans. Catering to traffic from the airport and Dixie Downs Speedway, the place was so close to Anthony's house he could have driven here nearly as fast as finding a free elevator to get down to the first floor.

But Tess Hardaway was somewhere in this hotel, and he'd waste valuable hunting time if he had to drive back and forth every day. He planned to make the most of every chance to cross her path this weekend.

Once he finally caught her.

Grabbing the convention program, Anthony sat on the edge of the bed and studied the hotel map to get a lay of the land. All the hospitality suites were located on the second floor, promoting sponsors who'd paid big bucks to have their names appear in the brochure that would go to twenty-six hundred conventioneers and car enthusiasts from all over the world.

Anthony knew every one of the advertisers. Automotive suppliers. Major manufacturers. Classic car restorers. He'd even heard of the new car dealerships. Only the biggest and best could afford to host events and advertise in Nostalgic Car Club's slick promotional program.

Turning the booklet over, he wondered what an ad in here would cost. Hell, what about the price of hosting a weekend hospitality suite for twenty-six hundred guests?

Ten, twenty grand?

While he could have afforded to spend that kind of money on advertising, this wasn't his market. His business might have grown into New Orleans's most reputable service and maintenance center in the years since he'd opened the doors, but vehicle owners wouldn't travel from Maine or Washington state to have their car tuned up at Anthony DiLeo Automotive.

This sort of promotion only benefited the big boys.

Over the past few years, Anthony had watched Auto-CarTex become a big boy. The used-car dealership had expanded its operation by opening new service centers all over the nation, growing slowly, steadily, *successfully*. If he hooked up with Tess Hardaway, he'd take a step toward becoming a big boy, too.

With that thought, he rolled up the program, stuffed it into his back pocket and headed downstairs.

He found AutoCarTex's hospitality suite easily enough. People had already begun milling through, glancing at the full-color advertising spreads detailing AutoCarTex's unique philosophy on used vehicles as they worked their way toward the buffet.

Anthony wasn't interested in food. He was interested in the woman dressed in a dark blue business suit working the crowd.

Tess Hardaway?

He couldn't catch her name badge from this distance but in that getup, she had to be with the company. He'd already had his fill of dealing with the AutoCarTex corporate types in his quest to get to the man who'd founded the company—Big Tex Hardaway.

Now those fruitless dealings had brought him to this convention to track down the man's only daughter.

But as he neared the woman, Anthony second-guessed himself. From what he'd read about Tess Hardaway, he'd expected someone less…*suit*, precisely the reason he'd chosen her.

He waited. The woman didn't take long to direct her guests to the buffet, and when she had, she extended her hand to him.

"Penny Parker of AutoCartex." Her name badge read Marketing Director.

A *serious* suit.

"Anthony DiLeo of Anthony DiLeo Automotive."

She had an easy smile and a sharp gaze that took him in all at once. "A business owner. Local?"

He inclined his head.

"Please tell me you're not worried that AutoCarTex's Louisiana expansion will cut into your bottom line."

Anthony laughed. "I happen to respect smart business strategy, and Big Tex's makes sense. He has made reliable used transportation more accessible. I think that's a good thing."

"Even when we open an auto showroom in your backyard?

"My service center is well established in town. I don't have anything to worry about."

Her expression suggested she approved his answer, and he continued, not above showing at least one of AutoCarTex's suits that this auto mechanic was made of more than they seemed to think. "Too many people treat cars as if they're disposable. Consumers pay through the nose to drive a new car out of the showroom when an older one only needs a little TLC."

"You sound like a spokesperson for AutoCarTex, Mr. DiLeo."

That made him smile. "Anthony."

"All right, Anthony," she said with just enough drawl to tell him she was Southern. "If you didn't come to pick my brain about our new showroom, then what can I do for you? Interested in our mission statement? Our involvement with the Nostalgic Car Club? How about our service warranty contract?"

"I'm looking for Tess Hardaway. I heard she'd be around."

"Really? Do you know Tess?"

"Not personally."

"I'm afraid you just missed her."

"I seem to be doing that a lot today."

That sharp gaze cut across him again, seemed to notice there was more here than met the eye. And she clearly hadn't decided if *that* was good.

"You don't happen to know where she went, do you?"

Penny leaned back on her stylish pumps and folded her arms across her chest. "Normally, I wouldn't dream of asking, but something about your interest is smacking of more personal than professional. Why do you want to see Tess?"

"I'm sorry if I gave you that impression, Ms. Parker."

"Penny, please."

"Penny. My interest is strictly business. I came to this convention to network with Ms. Hardaway."

"Are you interested in the AutoCarTex Foundation?"

"So to speak." That wasn't entirely true, but close enough. "I'd rather keep my business between me and Ms. Hardaway."

"Now I'm intrigued. Not even a hint?"

He spread his hands in entreaty. "Nothing mysterious. Just business."

She eyed him again. He got the impression she couldn't quite make out what a local service center owner might want with the director of the AutoCarTex Foundation, which dealt with the public relations and charitable donations parts of the corporation. He also got the impression *her* interest was more than professional.

"She went to the speedway for the race."

"What race?" he asked. "I thought the convention didn't start until the welcome reception tonight."

"It doesn't *officially* start, but we always kick off with a low-speed race. Gets everyone in the mood. Tess wouldn't miss it for the world. Didn't you read your itinerary?"

"Not closely enough." He extended his hand. "A pleasure meeting you, Penny. Looks like I'm off to the races. I'm sure I'll run into you again."

She shook with a firm grip. "If you don't catch up with her, try back here later. She'll be in and out all weekend."

"Thanks."

Anthony left the hotel optimistic that he might finally catch the woman who'd been eluding him all day. His optimism lasted until he reached the speedway ticket booth.

"Gates closed to the public," a grizzled man wearing a Dixie Downs uniform told him.

"I'm attending the convention."

"Name badge? Driving pass?"

Damn it. "In my hotel room. I didn't know I needed them."

"Can't let you through without your name badge and your driving pass."

A car stopped at the nearby booth, flashed some papers and drove through the gates.

"I won't be driving, just watching."

The gate didn't budge.

"When does the race start?"

The ticket-taker glanced at his watch. "Ten minutes."

Not enough time to get to and from the hotel and still search the crowds for Tess Hardaway before the race began. He didn't think she'd be hard to find, though. Probably in the stands with the event hosts. "Can you call someone with the convention to verify I'm registered?"

"Call who?" the man asked gruffly, clearly not thrilled that Anthony intended to give him a hard time. Cocking his grizzled head toward the parking lot beyond the gate, he said, "The whole car club is inside for the race."

Anthony thought about dropping Penny Parker's name, but decided against it. The woman had been skeptical enough about his interest in Tess. "The volunteer working the registration desk will confirm I'm with the convention—"

"I got my orders."

"What about the hotel? They have me checked in with the car club's room block."

"Name badge and driving pass. It says so in the rules." He flourished a copy of Big Banger and Bourbon Street's program.

"But I—"

"Name badge and driving pass," the ticket-taker repeated stubbornly. "Or I call security."

First impressions were everything and being labeled a gate-crasher by speedway security was *not* the first impression Anthony wanted to make with Big Tex's daughter. The success of his new career path now depended on her.

Scowling, he shifted his car into Reverse and backed out of the ticket booth. It wasn't until he'd almost reached the road that a sign caught his eye.

Drivers.

Anthony was New Orleans born and bred. He might not have belonged to a fancy car club like Nostalgic until he'd wanted to meet Tess Hardaway, but he'd been around cars since he could sit up straight enough to be strapped into his dad's vintage GTO.

Even more importantly, he'd been hanging around Dixie Downs for nearly as long. His first paying job had been in the pit working for a locally sponsored team. He knew his way around.

Without another thought, Anthony bypassed the gate

and wheeled his car down the road leading to the track. He slid into the queue as if he belonged there.

When he reached the crewman in charge of registering the racers, he cranked down his window and said, "I'm looking for Tess Hardaway."

The guy didn't even look up over his clipboard. "The pole."

Well, well, well. He'd been wrong. Tess Hardaway wasn't in the stands, after all. She was lined up to race.

Leaning out his open window, he craned to see around the queue to the course and spotted her immediately. One look and every bit of his inner car enthusiast cringed.

A *Gremlin?* A *purple* Gremlin.

He couldn't miss the florid paint, the custom parts or the jacked-up rear tires turning the classic that had inspired the phrase "What happened to the rest of your car?" into a hot rod to shake the streets. The driver wore a matching purple helmet.

He smiled. Here he'd been worried about first impressions. Anthony had to wonder if Tess Hardaway would want to know his first impression of her. He doubted it.

"Where's your gear?" The crewman had finally glanced up from his clipboard. "Can't give you a number without your gear."

"In the trunk." He'd expected to race sometime this weekend and now seemed as good a time as any to start. Hopping out, he circled his car, hoping he didn't need anything more than a helmet and gloves.

The crewman gave a nod. "We're running with the National Racing Council rule book. Helmet will work today, but if you want to race in Saturday's high-speed autocross, you'll need a fire suit."

"Got it."

The crewman must have assumed Anthony had shown his name badge and driving pass at the gate because he slapped a number twenty-one inside the windshield and waved him through. The next thing Anthony knew, he slipped into the third row of the grid to wait for the pace car.

He finally had Tess Hardaway in sight.

Pulling on his helmet, he revved the engine to drown out the low-slung Corvette showing off in the slot beside him.

Classic car owners could be a competitive bunch, and he easily admitted that he was no different. But in Anthony's experience Corvette owners were the worst. Elitists.

A past president of the local Corvette club had officially endorsed Anthony's service center as the place to cater to the classic crowd. Ever since, he had been servicing the bulk of their members, most of whom thought they were doing him a favor by letting his staff touch their showy wheels. Some even tried to make him see the error of his Pontiac-driving ways.

This Corvette looked mint, but his own first-generation Firebird had a 400-cubic-inch V-8. He'd personally disabled the manufacturer's device that kept the engine from reaching full throttle. His Firebird would dominate that black Corvette before they'd pulled through the second lap.

Anthony might not have raced in a while, but his foot slipped onto the gas pedal instinctively when the pace car appeared to lead them around the track for a parade lap. One by one the cars pulled out to give the spectators a good look at the lineup.

Then came a pace lap before the official start of the

race. The drivers traveled in formation, steadily increasing speed until they hit the ceiling before the starting line.

Then came the flag.

Anthony's adrenaline shot into gear with his engine. The Dixie Downs Speedway was his course. He knew the groove by heart—when to shut off to negotiate banked turns, what turns to ride the rails. He knew when to lean into the accelerator to gain distance through the chutes.

His Firebird took to the track as if he'd just raced her yesterday, and when the black Corvette tried to shut him out, Anthony diced a little, forcing the Corvette to back off.

He blew past with a laugh, his fingers easily gripping the steering wheel. He sailed past a mint-condition Camaro. No contest. The Firebird had been designed to outrun the Chevy. It had been too long since he'd done anything that had gotten his blood pumping like this.

Too damned long.

His fellow contestants didn't stand a chance. Anthony had a Gremlin to catch, and a driver leading the pack.

The feel of the track beneath his wheels and the silky way his car handled each turn brought back memories of the innumerable times he'd raced here. With his dad when he'd been alive. With his brother Marc, who had such a serious need for speed that their mother swore he'd given her every gray hair she kept meticulously dyed. When Anthony had worked in the pit, making passes around this track in his employers' cars to clock some wickedly fast times.

Now each lap brought him closer to that purple hot rod.

Finally, he slipped into place behind her. After a few laps on her tail, Anthony admitted that not only did her funky little Gremlin pack more rpm grunt than he'd expected, but Tess Hardaway was one damned skilled driver. A little ruthless even.

She clearly enjoyed the thrill of the chase because she kept blipping to make him adjust his speed. Anthony let her play him for a bit. He intended to ride her bumper straight to the finish line. This woman would *not* get away again.

But the more she toyed with him, the harder he found it not to toy back.

Instinct finally took over. Slipping into her draft, he followed closely enough to take advantage of the decreased air resistance, so close that the chrome Gremlin character on her hatch grinned wickedly like a dare.

The race was on.

He sped up.

She slowed down.

He maneuvered the track.

She shut him out so he couldn't pass.

While Anthony might not have Tess Hardaway's maneuvers, he had the better car. And he put his Firebird to work when she fishtailed out of a hairy turn. She controlled the motion instantly—testimony to her skill—but skill was the only thing carrying her right now.

Instinct told him her hot rod was full out while his V-8 still had more to give. With a little more grunt and a lot of luck, he could maneuver past, well before that checkered flag came down to signal the end of the race.

Anthony had a split second to decide.

Whipping this woman's butt on the track hardly seemed a better introduction than being dragged in by security for crashing the gate.

But even more important than making a good first impression was the question: could Anthony live with himself if he let that prissy purple Gremlin whip *his* butt?

THE FIREBIRD DRAFTED Tess all the way down the chute. She couldn't shake him. Although she drove with her pedal to the metal, this muscle car clung to her bumper as though it had been painted on. And the second she misjudged a banked turn, it broke out of her draft to slingshot around and take the lead.

Now it was Tess's turn to ride a bumper. But what a bumper it was. The shiny chrome and gleaming taillights blurred as the Firebird drifted into the chute, a neat, controlled slide that sealed the deal about who would win this race.

The distance between them lengthened as they neared the checkered flag. Her five-liter engine might give her lightweight Gremlin a lively performance, but it couldn't touch what this driver had growling beneath his hood.

And she had to give him credit for not stroking all the way to the finish line. He could have rubbed her loss in her face by slowing down when he knew she couldn't catch up, but once he took the lead, he ran with it.

As long as he was winning, he would win big. As far as Tess was concerned that sort of confidence said something about a driver. And by the time she wheeled into the pit lane, she wanted to know who he was.

She didn't recognize the red Firebird with the white hardtop and gleaming chrome side pipes. Removing her helmet, she handed it to the volunteer who had been assigned to her pit and treated herself to a deep breath of fuel-tinged summer air. *Mmm-mmm.* There was nothing like it.

"Well now," a familiar voice drawled. "There's a sight you don't see every day. Tess Hardaway in the number two spot."

She turned to find a coworker strolling toward her on grossly expensive Italian pumps. "What are you doing in my pit? Your hair will smell like exhaust fumes."

Penny ran a manicured hand over her smooth black bob and patted it in place. "Can't be helped."

"Why's that? And aren't you supposed to be working the hospitality suite?"

She nodded. "I passed the ball to our resident over-achiever. He was happy to do his bit for the cause."

This overachiever was the AutoCarTex Foundation's newest employee, and Tess's personal assistant, Hal. The new graduate could make typing a letter seem worthy of his business degree from a prestigious northeastern university. That knack had won him the job. His enthusiasm felt contagious, and she appreciated anyone who could spread it like butter around her office.

"I'll bet," she said. "Just don't take advantage of my assistant. I need him this weekend. All I've been doing is putting out fires. Nothing's coming together."

"I'll say." Penny laughed. "We'll be able to hear your Uncle Ray hooting from Texas when he finds out you lost a race. So who did the honors?"

Tess glanced to where the driver of the Firebird had pulled before the stand to accept his trophy. "Whoever's driving that Firebird. My money's on a local. He knew the track."

But Penny didn't respond. She was too busy staring at the man who emerged from the winning car. Even from this distance, Tess could make him out as a tall, very well-built man who filled out his jeans nicely. He pulled off his helmet to reveal tawny blond hair that waved back from his face, long enough that he'd tied it in a small ponytail.

"That's Anthony DiLeo. You're right. He's a local."

No surprise there. "Who is he?"

"A service shop owner who's apparently so well established, he's not in the least bit worried about us cutting into his business when we open our new showroom in town."

No surprise there, either. The man drove confident, which meant he must be confident.

Penny shot her one of *those* expressions, one that declared something was up. "He came to the hospitality suite looking for you. Said he'd been missing you all day."

"What does he want?"

"Business. Wouldn't say what kind. Thought I'd give you the heads-up."

Tess would have to be deaf to miss the innuendo in that statement. "Are you worried?"

"About this man? No. I liked him, but I did promise your father I'd stay on red alert so the wack job du jour doesn't get anywhere near his precious baby."

"Give it a rest, Penny."

"Your father's worried, Tess. He doesn't want you driving the rally alone, and I can't say I blame him. So don't shoot the messenger. I'm just doing my job."

This was a tired excuse Tess had heard all too often. "Last I heard you were a marketing director, not a babysitter."

"With any other company the roles would be mutually exclusive. Not at *your* company, though. According to your father part of my job is watching your back, as you well know."

Boy, did she ever. Shielding the late-afternoon sun from her eyes, Tess watched Anthony DiLeo toss his helmet inside his car. Nope, she'd never seen him before. She wouldn't have forgotten a man who walked like that, long legs chewing up the track with possessive strides. And his car…that was one well-kept muscle car. She wondered if he'd restored it himself.

"No clue what he wants?"

Penny shook her head. "None. But I'll be disappointed if he turns out to be the latest wack job. He is one handsome man."

"Wouldn't know," Tess said dryly. "I've only seen him with his helmet on when he passed me on the track."

"Then take my word for it. This one's yummy."

"You said the same thing about Daryl Keene."

"That one's yummy, too."

Tess rubbed her temples. If she could just rub away Penny as easily. But no matter where she turned lately, she ran smack into someone her daddy had sent to watch her back.

"You know, it's not so bad having people look out for you," Penny admonished.

Spoken by someone whose back wasn't being watched. Tess leaned against the railing and met Penny's scowl. "Do you know how many people work at AutoCarTex headquarters? That's *a lot* of back watchers. My daddy is on the wrong side of overprotective on a good day, and he's gone off the deep end lately."

Penny's scowl faded fast. "I had no idea the commercials would turn into a trail of bread crumbs for the crazies."

"You couldn't have foreseen the problem. None of us

could. Most of Johnny Q. Public thinks Daddy is their best friend. And look at all the good the commercials have done. Not only for corporate but for the Foundation."

"I still feel responsible. I dreamed up the promotional campaign. And these letters your father's been getting lately have him really worried. This latest one is threatening family and friends along with the accusations of gross capitalism."

Boy, did Tess know all about that. Daddy hadn't been this worked up since she'd gone to the movies on her first date with that cute hand from the Critchley ranch.

"Do you think this one's trouble?" She glanced at Anthony DiLeo as he exchanged greetings with the car club's president.

"He didn't strike me as a crazy, but he wants something."

"Who doesn't? Another side effect of Daddy's success, and one you're not responsible for."

Penny gave a low whistle. "If you don't mind my saying, Tess, every drop of blood in your veins will turn to prairie dust if you don't have some fun. *Soon.*"

How much fun could she have when all of AutoCar-Tex's employees kept their eyes on her at work? Daddy and Uncle Ray tag-teamed at home, and dropping by her apartment unexpectedly and checking out her friends were both time-consuming jobs. She knew they had more important things to do than babysit her, so by necessity, Tess limited her activities.

This hadn't proven much of a problem lately. Except for the convention, her schedule had been keeping her pretty close to home. And she hadn't met any man who seemed worthy of checking out in a while.

"Penny, I'll date again just as soon as I come across a man who isn't more interested in Daddy than me."

"What could Daryl Keene possibly want?" Penny sidled up to her and peered down the track to where the man himself directed the pit crew's efforts with his black Corvette. "His daddy is richer than your daddy."

Tess grudgingly followed her gaze. All right, she couldn't argue finances. Or appearance, either. Daryl Keene had been cut from a very handsome mold. Tall, polished looking with his neat black hair and slick smiles.

"I don't know. But he wants something or else he wouldn't still be hounding me for a date. He's even started e-mailing me through my corporate account. And now he's checking out a dealership in Lubbock. He told me he's heading up the project so he can spend more time in town."

"Sure you're not paranoid? Sounds like he doesn't want more than to get inside your size-four jeans. You should go to dinner or a movie. Something *fun.*"

Tess rolled her eyes. "Not interested."

"But why? Your daddy knows his daddy, so he probably doesn't even need to run a background check on the guy. Not to mention he's downright yummy."

"He's a trailer queen."

"Who cares if he hauls his car or drives it? He's cute, and rich to boot."

Tess bit back a smile at Penny's criteria. "Honestly, I can't take Daryl up on his offer."

"Why not? I'm talking dinner here, not marriage and two-point-five kids. Give me a reason that's based in reality."

"No sparks. Not a one."

Penny considered that for a minute then pushed away from the rail with a heavy sigh. "Damn shame that."

Although Tess didn't consider Daryl much of a loss, it had been so long since she'd felt sparks for any man she'd begun to wonder if it wasn't a hormonal thing. Did the libido die down the closer one got to thirty?

She couldn't bring herself to ask Penny, who was around her age. While they were friendly, Penny was a career gal well aware of who approved her every step up the corporate ladder. The last thing Tess needed was her daddy getting wind of any medical concerns. Maybe she'd do some Internet research. This might be something a few herbal supplements could cure.

Or maybe Penny was right, and she was paranoid. But Tess had a right to be cautious. Most men weren't interested *in* her, but in *using* her, a problem she'd first encountered long ago, while dating a man from upper management at AutoCarTex Corporate.

Everyone seemed to want to get close to her daddy.

"The winner of Big Banger and Bourbon Street's first race is new car club member Anthony DiLeo." The car club's president rescued her from more self-analysis when he spoke over the microphone. "To celebrate his win, Mr. DiLeo is making a generous ten-thousand-dollar cash contribution to the Children's Hope League in the name of his service center, Anthony DiLeo Automotive of New Orleans, Louisiana."

The crowd roared approval and Penny said, "Well, well, well. Looks like my instincts are on target. Anthony DiLeo isn't striking me as your run-of-the-mill wacko."

"That remains to be seen."

"Sour grapes. You can't win every race. At least hear what the man has to say."

Tess didn't have to hear him speak a word—she already knew what he was up to. "He's sucking up."

"What makes you say that?"

"We're sponsoring the Children's Hope League this year."

"And AutoCarTex is the only corporation contributing to this charity?"

"Of course not," she huffed. "But I'm guessing he's contributing to this charity because we are. The man definitely wants something. I want to know what it is."

2

APPARENTLY ANTHONY DiLEO wanted her. He glanced Tess's way as soon as he left the stand, and after tossing his grand-prize trophy carelessly into the back seat, he hopped into his idling car and headed toward them.

Tess watched as he backed across the track in a quick, clean move, and she had to admit that while his driving skill clearly wasn't a result of formal training, he had a natural ability that impressed her.

Pulling to a sharp stop, he left exactly enough room to open his door and clear the rail separating them. Another smooth move probably meant to impress. She had to admit—at least to herself—that it did. But not nearly as much as the man who stepped out of the car.

He unfolded a lean, mean body in an energetic burst of strength that made her stare, starting at the butter-soft-looking leather slip-ons he wore with no socks. Nicely muscled thighs did even better things to his jeans up close, and his neat cotton shirt hinted at some serious definition below. And when she finally made it to his face…

Tess had already guessed by the name that something about this man would be Italian. But one glimpse into his handsome face confirmed that not something, but *everything* screamed his heritage. Deep olive skin. Strong, carved features that contrasted strikingly with golden-brown bedroom eyes that checked her out as thoroughly as she did him.

His gaze swept across her like a warm breeze, a physical sensation, and the *only* thing to remind her to breathe again.

His hair was too long to be considered anything but rebellious, yet it was a tawny touchable blond. And his smile… This man had a kissing mouth, plain and simple, because there was no way Tess could look at that wide mouth and not think about kissing.

She had to shake her head to clear *that* thought away.

Whoa! Anthony DiLeo had chemistry with a capital *C* and he blasted it all over her. And that knowing smile assured her she wasn't the only one thinking about kissing right now, either.

Then he reached over the railing and took her hand.

His handshake should have been perfectly professional, but the instant their fingers met, Tess knew she wouldn't need any herbs to jump-start her libido. Touching this man did the trick nicely. He had working hands. Rough skin here and there. And danged if she didn't vibrate a little when his warm, strong fingers finally slipped away.

"Ms. Hardaway, I've been hoping to meet you." His voice was all whiskey smooth and lazy bayou, a sound that strummed her insides like a guitar under a starry sky.

"So I've heard." The crazily breathless sound of her voice came as another surprise.

And made Penny snort with laughter behind her.

Tess had forgotten Penny was even there, but a glance over her shoulder proved she was still watching Tess's back. The look on her face screamed smug amusement, which did a lot to help Tess get a grip on her brushfire re-action to this man.

"What can I do for you?" She took a step back, amazed by what a little distance did to slow her racing pulse.

After nodding in greeting to Penny, Anthony slid his warm gaze back to her. "I hoped for some of your time this weekend. I have some business to discuss."

"See what I mean about this cryptic stuff?" Penny might have sounded wary, but she eyed the man as if he were the last finger-licking-good drumstick.

"Is that why you made such a generous contribution to the charity I'm sponsoring this year, Mr. DiLeo? Were you hoping to score points so I'd make time for you?"

Hooking an arm over his car door, Anthony DiLeo looked at her evenly, and his expression suggested he didn't mind her candor. "I wanted to make a good first impression."

"You could have stayed behind her on the track," Penny said. "That would have worked."

He laughed, a rich rolling sound that sent another shock wave through Tess. "If I could have, I would have."

"Why couldn't you?" Tess asked, curious.

"I've got this thing about looking myself in the mirror and respecting what I see. I couldn't let you win when I knew I could. I hoped my contribution would make up for the slight."

Tess backed away, needing more distance between them to reason this through. "You didn't want to lose to a woman?"

"No. I have zero problem with you being a woman." That gaze of his raked along her body, proving his point louder than words ever could. "I didn't want to lose to a *purple Gremlin.*"

Penny hooted with laughter. "Calling Tess's baby ugly is *not* the way to make friends."

He lifted those broad shoulders in an apologetic shrug. "I didn't say ugly. But I'd be lying if I said that maniacal grinning Gremlin didn't provoke me a little."

"Another man who's attached to his car," Penny said. "But this one's no trailer queen, I'll bet."

Anthony DiLeo let his grimace speak for him, drawing her attention back to his striking features, and the way her stomach swooped every time she met his bedroom gaze.

She couldn't be *this* attracted to a nutter, could she?

No. This man might have a big car and an ego to match, but she had an internal alarm that was even bigger. She could spot a sidewinder from a mile off—had certainly honed her skills—and while Anthony DiLeo might want something from her, he'd been shooting straight so far.

"What sort of business did you want to discuss? Penny told me that you're a service center owner here in town. You do realize I'm with the AutoCarTex Foundation, don't you?"

"I did my research, Ms. Hardaway."

"Is that how you knew I'd be racing today?"

He shook his head, and she couldn't help but notice the way his hair glinted. Thick, silky hair that was the most incredible color, like a sun-washed echo of his golden-brown eyes. "Penny was kind enough to give me that information. She took pity on me because I've been chasing you all afternoon."

"The hotel was the only place you couldn't catch her," Penny said. "Another hint, Anthony. Tess isn't used to losing on the race track."

He waved a hand dismissively, and she noticed he wore

no ring on his third finger. "Not with her skill, but I had the edge. I've been racing this track since I learned to drive."

"So you don't think you're a better driver?"

"Penny!"

Anthony laughed. "Like I said, I had the edge. My car's bigger, too."

"I'm warming to him, Tess. He didn't come right out and say you're a better driver, but he knows it."

"What does this have to do with anything?" she asked.

Penny elbowed Tess playfully, but her eyes swept over the man as if she wanted to lick her fingers. "Shows a man's character, I think. His ego's not so fragile that he has to lie, but he's no pushover, either."

"I don't have any problems with my ego," he said.

No doubt. But Tess didn't miss how diplomatic he was, which she thought said a lot about him, too.

She wished she could see inside that handsome head to know what he was thinking. He'd tracked her down to discuss some sort of business and wound up with Penny inspecting him like a breeder. She wondered what Anthony DiLeo thought of all the innuendo pouring off her companion right now.

Tess knew what she thought—that this was the grossest display of unprofessionalism she'd ever seen. And Penny would hear about it as soon as they were alone again.

But until she could voice that opinion, she would run interference, which meant ending this interview. "I enjoyed the competition. I'll make some time to talk this weekend."

"I'm at your convenience, Ms. Hardaway. Just name the time and the place."

"I'm afraid tonight's a bust. The board is throwing a dinner for the presenters."

"What about tomorrow morning?" Penny suggested.

"No go." Tess shook her head. "I'm moderating the panel discussion during breakfast."

Anthony waited patiently while she mentally worked through her schedule.

Penny wasn't so patient. "Why don't you give me Hal to set up at the park? I doubt the hospitality suite will have much traffic with everyone getting ready for the caravan. You can slip away and meet Anthony for coffee."

"That'll work. Hotel coffee shop around eleven?"

Anthony nodded. "I'll be there."

With bells on, if Tess read the smile right.

ANTHONY TOOK ONE LOOK at the babe sprawled on the classic car's hood and knew he'd been plunked into the mother of all fantasies. He also understood why *Auto Coupe Magazine* had featured a purple AMC Gremlin in its annual calendar. This babe could make any car look good. Even this one.

She had a mane of glossy brown hair that tumbled sexily around her shoulders. She leaned back on her hands, which thrust her breasts proudly forward, and hiked one of her long bare legs on the hood. The other draped down in front of a headlight, dangling an ultrafeminine sandal from her foot. Her neat toenails were painted a pale pink that strangely complimented the garish purple paint.

Then again, with this babe showcasing the car, who really cared what color the car was?

Not Anthony. Not when the calendar babe wore a matching pink muscle shirt in some clingy fabric that hugged her full breasts so close that he could see the out-line of her nipples.

She wasn't wearing a bra.

The silky shorts didn't leave much to the imagination, either—except to inspire thoughts of how he could peel them down her legs....

With his hands while stroking her soft thighs.

With his teeth while nibbling her creamy skin.

With *her* hands while she performed a fantasy strip-tease.

Yeah. He liked the idea of Calendar Babe stripping for him.

But when had *Auto Coupe Magazine* turned his garage into a photo set?

Sure enough when Anthony looked around, the purple Gremlin with its lovely model was parked smack in the middle of his twenty bays, and he didn't have a clue how they'd gotten there. His head couldn't fit the pieces to-gether, and his body didn't care. Not when Calendar Babe had come to life.

Propping herself up on one hand, she brought a mani-cured finger to her lips, drawing his attention to how ripe her glossy mouth was for kissing.

Oh, yeah!

Then she trailed that finger down her throat…down…down. Hooking it inside the scooped neck of her muscle shirt, she drew his gaze like a magnet to the creamy swell of her cleavage, the rise of luscious breasts on an excited breath.

Then she dragged the shirt down.

Full swells of pale skin spilled out in a tumble, riding high over the straining collar. The sight stole the breath from his lungs. His dick shot to about one degree below a crippling erection. He clutched the doorjamb tighter.

Her rose-colored nipples were darker than he'd imagined, the tips harder than he'd hoped.

Anthony *had* died and gone to heaven.

Calendar Babe heaven.

Suddenly, her foot stopped in middangle, dragging his gaze from those lush breasts to the sandal suspended from her toes. She let it fall to the floor. He knew the wooden heel must have made some sound on the concrete, but he couldn't hear a thing past the blood throbbing in his ears.

Then she drew her long legs underneath her and spun around, an erotic display of motion that turned the car hood into a dance floor. Her arms lifted gracefully. Her breasts bounced sexily. She rose up on her knees so he could admire her in profile. Then she began rocking her hips back and forth.

And working those pink shorts down, down, down.

Anthony watched, his breath stalling as the curve of a slim hip appeared. Inch by inch, more creamy skin became visible…the tight curve of her butt…the sleek line of her thigh…and Anthony realized…Calendar Babe went commando.

"Will you pull it out for me, Anthony?"

It?

In some dim part of his brain, Anthony knew Calendar Babe's Texas twang should have been familiar. But for the life of him, he couldn't remember why. How in hell was he supposed to think when she dropped that emerald gaze to his crotch?

It.

He was game. Hell, it seemed only fair to return the favor when she performed so eagerly for him. Unzipping his fly, he slid his pants down on his hips, carefully maneuvering his erection away from the zipper.

"Will you stroke it for me? I want to see you get hard."

Get hard? He was as stiff as a steering column.

But he wouldn't deny her anything. Wrapping his fingers around himself, he gave a slow tug. Then another.

She pursed her lips and blew him a kiss. "Mmm, you are hard, big boy. Come here."

Sliding the shorts over her knees, she kicked them off her feet. Then she slithered off the hood and stood in all her barely clad glory.

For a minute, Anthony could do nothing but stare. She posed in front of the car, bare bottomed, breasts still popping over her collar in a stunning display of nipple and skin.

Then she flashed him an inviting smile. The eagerness he saw in her face, in those deep green eyes that were almost too green to be real, was enough to propel him into motion.

He wouldn't miss this fantasy.

She extended her hand to him as he approached, and the feel of her fingertips slipping around his erection, drawing him to her, was the last proof Anthony needed to know he'd indeed died and gone to heaven.

He went to pull her into his arms, but she tightened her grip on his dick, used it as a handle to steer him to the car. Then she pushed him toward the hood.

"Sit."

He could barely think let alone argue. So he hoisted himself onto the hood, watching in amazement as she bent low over him, her mouth replacing her hand….

She swirled her tongue over him in a warm velvet stroke. His dick jumped, bumping against her shiny pink lips.

She laughed, a delightful silvery sound. "Oh, Anthony."

She moved in for the kill.

Her mouth became a suck zone, drawing him in, one long pull that made him tingle from his toes to the roots of his hair. A growl spilled from his mouth, a sound that echoed off the garage walls, the sound of appreciation.

Spearing his fingers into her hair, Anthony hung on while she took him for a ride, head bobbing, tongue swirling, those glossy pink lips in a liplock that could have sucked the chrome off his bumper.

Somewhere in the rational part of his brain, Anthony knew her lipstick should have long ago smeared. But those enticing lips remained as glossy and perfect as they had when this fantasy began, and he couldn't spare even a brain cell to reason through the phenomenon.

Not when he couldn't keep his fingers from threading deeper into her hair, urging her to quicken the pace. Not when he couldn't stop arching his hips to press back inside her warm mouth.

He hovered in that twilight moment—about to explode but unable to let himself go because the fantasy would be over.

Calendar Babe must have read his mind because she slipped her hand under his balls and fondled him. Her shiny lips parted, and she twirled a hot wet lick around the head of his dick.

She slipped her fingers between his legs and whispered, "I hear this is the male G-spot."

Slithering a moist finger backward…

Anthony opened his eyes and stared blindly at the bedside clock. It took forever to make sense of what he was seeing—a digital display that read 3:14 a.m.

Still eight hours before he met with the woman who'd just made an appearance in the most erotic dream he'd ever had. And as he lay on the hard hotel bed with every nerve in his body firing like a new spark plug, Anthony got the sinking feeling that eight hours and an icy shower weren't going to take the edge off the effects of *that* dream any time soon.

ANTHONY ARRIVED at the hotel's coffee shop early enough to locate a table reasonably removed from the traffic. After ordering a big cup of joe with a few extra shots of espresso thrown in to clear his head, he booted his laptop, organized his spreadsheets for easy access and took a few gulps of the supercharged brew.

He needed the extra caffeine after spending the remainder of his night too keyed up to sleep. His brain had replayed that incredible dream, and when Tess strolled through the door a few minutes after eleven, Anthony knew he was in trouble. *Big* trouble. The sight of her hit him every place it counted.

She moved with a light, purposeful grace. She wasn't exactly tall, but she was willowy and slim, which made her appear that way. He hadn't gotten close enough yet to tell for sure, but he thought the top of her head might reach his chin if they stood close.

The effect Tess was having on him came as a shock.

She might be one damn fine-looking woman, but Anthony knew many fine-looking women. There was something about her that made him think about sex in a way he hadn't in forever. Interested. Excited. And the feeling was about more than her glossy hair waving prettily around her face or those big eyes that were so deep a green they didn't seem real.

It wasn't the insane elf getup, either.

She'd dressed head to toe in red-and-green stripes for the Christmas in July caravan event. The short-shorts made him ogle her legs. Suspenders with blinking lights drew his gaze to her lean curves and left him wondering how he would conduct business when she looked like a Christmas present he wanted to unwrap.

Anthony had no good answer. He was completely aware of this woman and completely sandbagged by the feeling. He hadn't felt this sort of awareness for a woman since…hell, he'd only felt this punch-to-the-gut sort of awareness about *one woman*.

The woman he'd lost a long time ago.

"Good morning, Mr. DiLeo." Tess approached the table, all smooth moves and sultry Texas twang. "Please excuse the costume. AutoCarTex Foundation is sponsoring today's caravan. I'm headed there right after I meet with you."

He managed to pull his thoughts together in time to stand and slide out the chair for her. "Anthony, please. I appreciate you making the time to talk to me."

He appreciated another chance to get close. It had been so long since his body had shot into overdrive that he barely recognized the feeling.

Slipping into the chair, she sat down and eyed the table filled with his presentation gear. "I'll admit to being as curious as Penny about your business."

There was a breathless quality about her voice that had a similar effect on him. Chemistry. He'd been so caught up in his own yesterday that he hadn't been sure it worked both ways.

Today he was sure.

Motioning to the table between them, he said, "I

brought everything to show you but, first, can I get you coffee? Or something to eat? You worked through breakfast this morning."

"Yes, I did." She shot a glance at a glass case displaying high-calorie goodies and a tiny frown creased her brows.

"How about something to hold you over until lunch later?"

Anthony might not have belonged to any car enthusiast organization before this one, but he learned fast. When he hadn't been able to fall back asleep, he'd taken Timmy from Montgomery's advice and studied the itinerary. Now he was armed with enough information to know the caravan event would parade a long route through the city before arriving at a park for lunch. It would be hours yet before Tess's next meal.

She nodded. "Okay, thanks. A beignet and café au lait."

"Got it."

He headed toward the counter to place the order, pleased she'd taken him up on his suggestion. Now he'd have her undivided attention for at least as long as it took to eat.

He would play his hand straight with Tess. He'd prepared for months and wasn't about to let chemistry detour him from his course. He'd already learned the life lesson about letting his hormones rule his actions, and he'd learned it the hard way.

When Anthony returned to the table, he set the cup and plate in front of her and got straight to business. He had one shot to impress this woman with his business proposal, and spinning his laptop toward her, he maneuvered through windows to begin his PowerPoint presentation.

It was just a flashy overview of his business question,

but an impressive one, he thought. With photos taken in his own garage combined with stock photos of scenes from various AutoCarTex locations, he detailed facts about AutoCarTex's current service department situation and the numbers the company had reported for the past six quarters.

The situation in a nutshell: AutoCarTex sold used cars with service plans at affordable prices then maintained the cars to keep them running like new. Big Tex Hardaway's philosophy made reliable transportation available to the masses and his commitment to his customers had made AutoCarTex a household name.

The only flaw in Big Tex's smart business strategy was subcontracting his service centers, which made it hit-or-miss from dealership to dealership. The man's expertise clearly served him with sales and customer satisfaction, not in car maintenance.

That's where Anthony DiLeo Automotive came in.

He watched Tess sip her coffee as his proposed program—AutoTexCare—flashed across the screen. She looked politely interested but neutral as his presentation outlined what the plan would cover and how Anthony would standardize service in all AutoCarTex locations.

He could turn them into authorized service facilities and assets to the corporation—light-years stronger than the program currently in effect.

When the last slide concluded, he opened the folder. "I've brought along the numbers that support my projections."

Tess darted her tongue out to lick powdered sugar from her lips, and her gaze drifted to the spreadsheets. "Auto-TexCare, Anthony? You said you did your research. The

AutoCarTex Foundation handles public relations for my father's corporation, not automotive service. Why are you presenting your idea to me?"

"I've taken the conventional route through corporate channels," he said. "I haven't been able to get my proposal on the right desks. Your father's management staff doesn't seem interested in any ideas except those generated in-house."

Anthony knew that for a fact after spending five months being shuffled from desk to desk only to be told "Thanks but no thanks" in a form letter.

"I see. So Daddy's staff isn't interested in your idea."

"Afraid not."

"But you don't think he should subcontract his service work."

"I don't." Anthony slid the spreadsheet toward her for a better look. "It's all here in black and white. Subcontracting is the reason for these disparities in his year-to-date numbers. Of course I only had access to public record, but it's still easy to see that his service departments operate like wild cards, and he's using certain dealerships to carry others.

"It's ineffective. Your father breaks even on service, but give him a year or two when service dips into the red in too many locations, and his service plan becomes a liability. He'll be forced to divert profits from sales to balance the difference. Or to reconsider his service plan."

"But that plan is what makes AutoCarTex unique."

He nodded. As an industry insider, she knew the ups and downs of the car business and made his job easier with her knowledge. "With AutoTexCare, your father can standardize service and bring it consistently into the black. Like you said, his plan makes AutoCarTex unique. Reliable service should be a given in all his locations."

Tess toyed idly with her napkin and considered him for a moment. "Don't you think my daddy's staff is aware of all this?"

Anthony ignored the way she glanced up from beneath her lashes with those sultry green eyes and forced a diplomatic reply. "They're approaching the problem like corporate managers, not people who understand automotive service."

"They *are* corporate managers. And if that's a problem then whose desk do you think is the one to put your proposal on?"

"Your father's."

She inhaled deeply, visibly withdrawing into full professional mode, and while he didn't understand why she'd shut him down, he knew she had. "Well, I'm impressed with your research. You've obviously put a great deal of thought and effort into your proposal."

He'd worked on this proposal for six months before ever making the first overture toward AutoCarTex Corporate. His AutoTexCare plan represented his next career step.

And while gratified that Tess appreciated his effort, he'd also received enough polite dismissals to recognize another one coming. He cut her off at the pass. "I know coming to you is unconventional, but I've taken the normal route without success. Your public relations work for the AutoCarTex Foundation and your connection to Big Tex made you my best chance of success."

"You think you know what AutoCarTex needs better than the people Daddy pays?" Her Texas twang grew sharp around the edges. Her expression flared with challenge. Her green eyes gleamed.

"In this instance, yes. If your father would only take a look at my proposal, he'd agree."

She twirled a fingertip around the rim of her cup, drawing his gaze to the manicured pink tip no matter how hard he tried to stick to business. "You're very confident, Anthony. What makes you so sure Daddy will see your way on this?"

"Your father's employees might be capable corporate managers, but they don't have experience in running an automotive business. Your father does, and so do I. His expertise is in sales, mine's in service."

He'd plunked the situation squarely in her lap, forcing her to make a choice.

To help or not to help, that was the question.

One she wasn't sure how to answer. Her mood mirrored the sudden silence that became almost alive between them, an odd mixture of awareness and challenge.

"Wouldn't it just be simpler to sell franchises for your service center?" she finally asked. "Your name won't be in lights if you redesign Daddy's service departments. All your work will fall under the AutoCarTex umbrella."

"Seeing my name in lights isn't the point," he said, seizing the opportunity to prove he was focused strictly on business. "Reliable service is. My AutoTexCare plan offers that."

"Well, I certainly understand why Daddy's managers are having a problem with your proposal."

"Why's that?"

A smile tugged at the corners of her mouth. His question had clearly amused her, and something about that pricked his pride, made him feel as if *he'd* amused her.

"In order to implement your AutoTexCare plan, Daddy would have to create a new department to handle service. You're bypassing the corporate ladder, don't you think?"

"I'm qualified for the job. I have a degree in business."

"Perhaps, but the people on my daddy's team have climbed the rungs to their current positions in their careers."

"So have I. In my own corporation. I brought my company's prospectus along. You just have to take a look to see that I'm not bypassing anything. I've put in my time in the trenches. My experience servicing cars and running a business is what gives me the edge in pinpointing your father's needs."

"But why, Anthony? Why are you looking for a spot in my daddy's organization?"

"I believe in what he's doing." This was the *only* career move to spark his interest in a long time. "Your father is revolutionizing the automotive industry. I want to be a part."

"Revolutionizing, hmm? Interesting word choice. Are you looking for a thrill here?"

Ouch.

Damned if she didn't nail him on the story of his life. And after yesterday's race, he could have asked Tess Hardaway the same question. But the fact that she decided whether or not he was worth a recommendation made him keep his opinion to himself. He would be professional if it killed him. And when his gaze drifted to the red-and-green stripes stretching across her full breasts, Anthony knew it just might.

"My track record speaks for itself," he said instead. In business, and his personal life, which might explain the incredible awareness of this woman, everything from the way a tiny frown rode between her brows to the way she shifted slightly to hook her ankles beneath the table.

Why he felt *challenged* to convince her that his plan was worthy of a recommendation to her father.

"If you don't mind my asking, what's concerning you? You're a businesswoman. If you didn't see some potential in my proposal, you'd have already told me to take a hike."

"Do you have any idea how often I'm asked for introductions to my daddy?"

Ah, now they were getting somewhere.

"My idea is worth an introduction. If your father doesn't agree, I'm gone. No harm no foul. He stands to benefit, *a lot.*"

"So you say." Glancing at the spreadsheets between them, she left him to admire the silky black lashes that formed starbursts on her cheeks. "Not everyone is worth an introduction to my daddy. Ever since he started starring in the television promotional campaign, we've had all sorts of…*people* trying to contact him. Not all of them good."

He couldn't miss the subtext in that statement. "I'm not a stalker, Ms. Hardaway. Take a look at my credentials. I'm just a businessman who's out of options."

The tips of her mouth tucked up again, and she was fighting a smile, *amused* by him again. "I'll have to think about it, Anthony. That's the best I can do."

"It's not a no. And that means I have a chance to convince you I'm worth an introduction."

That challenge flared in those green depths again, unmistakable, but she effectively ended the conversation by glancing at her watch. "I'm not entirely sure what I'm setting myself up for, but I'm afraid I don't have any more time to discuss it. I've got to get to the lineup to talk with the police about any last-minute changes to the caravan route."

"I'll head over with you, if you don't mind." He quickly shoveled papers inside the folder and powered down his laptop.

"You're registered? I don't recall your name on the list."

Shoving his laptop inside the case, he tossed the spreadsheets on top. "I registered this morning."

"If you're driving in a Christmas in July caravan, don't you think you should dress the part? And your car, too."

"The paint's red. Does that count?"

"Hmm." Her mouth pursed in a contemplative moue. "I might have something that'll work."

"I'd appreciate it." Gathering up his things, Anthony followed her out of the coffee shop.

The Gremlin was a bizarre-looking car on a good day—he would have never called a lady's car ugly—but decorated with red-and-green garland and ropes of twinkling lights pushed it past bizarre into something downright alien.

And despite his decision not to let chemistry interfere with his plans for this woman, he found his resolve under attack every time she disappeared into the hatch, treating him to prime shots of her bottom in those striped shortshorts.

Anthony's pulse rate spiked accordingly, and he marveled at the speed and strength of his reaction. There'd only been one woman who'd ever possessed the ability to throw him onto red alert like this, one woman who'd dared him to reach beyond himself and strive to accomplish his goals.

And that had been so long ago he'd thought his ability to feel this sort of awareness dead and gone. Figured that it would crop back up exactly when it shouldn't.

"Here we go," Tess said. "Green garland to go with

your red paint. I used up all my lights, but I have this for the driver."

Draping green garland over her shoulder, she emerged from the car with a pair of brown felt antlers decorated with golden jingle bells. With a flip of a tiny switch, she showed him the best feature—blinking lights.

"You expect me to wear that." Not a question.

Leaning up on tiptoe, she dragged him from professional to personal in one liquid move. Suddenly she was so close he could smell her hair, fresh with an underlying hint of something sultry like vanilla or almond. Close enough to realize that the top of her head did indeed brush his chin. She slipped the antlers onto his head then stepped back to survey her handiwork.

He didn't need a mirror. Her facial contortions reflected his appearance better than a mirror could.

She was trying not to laugh.

"This is a character test, isn't it?"

Plucking the box from his arms, she deposited it back in her trunk. "We'll see how serious you are about impressing me."

"I can handle whatever you dish out, Ms. Hardaway."

She glanced back over her shoulder, a silky dark brow arched in question. "You're that sure?"

"Yes." The word came out sounding impressive, but inside Anthony didn't feel sure at all.

He didn't know how much longer he'd be able to resist slipping his arms around her, pulling her close and kissing that daring smile from her face.

3

Tess frowned into her rearview mirror at the man driving the parade route behind her. Anthony DiLeo maneuvered through the French Quarter streets keeping easy pace at this butt-numbing speed. The green garland streamers they'd wrapped around his car shimmered. He'd added a pair of stylish sunglasses to his costume, but even with a car length between them, she couldn't miss his antlered silhouette through the windshield.

So Anthony wanted to prove himself enough to let her dress him up like the Christmas goose?

That much determination said a lot about what he would do to gain her support for his cause, but this shouldn't come as a surprise. Been here, done this all before.

With one important difference—Anthony hadn't tried to put anything over on her.

He'd pursued her openly, stated his goal and how he intended to win her support. He hadn't finessed his way into her graces or manipulated an introduction. He'd been straightforward.

What wasn't so straightforward was her reaction to the man. Since the TV commercials had turned her smiling daddy into everyone's best friend, the rats had started crawling out of the woodwork with alarming frequency.

She'd met her fair share of men who wanted something from her, so this disappointment she was feeling didn't exactly make sense.

Why did she even care about Anthony DiLeo? Because he'd sparked life signs in her vacationing libido?

Maybe. Maybe not.

Mulling the question, Tess smiled at the police officer who'd blocked yet another intersection with his patrol car before she wheeled into the city park. She followed the parking attendants to rows reserved for the parade drivers.

Relieved for the chance to stretch, she parked and got out, waving to the crowd that had gathered along the sidelines to see the classic autos. She picked out Penny instantly, dressed smartly in a red-and-green pants suit that was bright enough to do justice to a Christmas in July event.

In her periphery, she saw Anthony emerge from his car and resisted the impulse to wait for him to catch up. She headed toward Penny instead. "I hope you don't melt in that getup. Didn't anyone tell you New Orleans gets hot in July?"

Penny smoothed the collar of her blouse, a poinsettia print number that complemented her slacks. "I represent AutoCarTex Corporate. I have to dress the part."

"And I don't?"

"You're the owner's daughter. You can get away with looking like one of Santa's elves."

"Good for me. I don't know how you stand there with this sun and not sweat."

"Good genes." She issued a low whistle. "And guess who's coming up the rear. The meeting go okay?"

Tess had only a chance to nod before Anthony appeared

behind her, his tall, broad self sucking up all the summery air with his maleness. Then came the blinding smile—clearly meant for her—and the responding flip-flop deep in her stomach that proved she was aware of him on a cellular level.

"Great antlers," Penny said.

"Christmas New Orleans style."

Tess wasn't sure what reindeer had to do with New Orleans, but before she had a chance to comment, her assistant showed up, looking frayed around the edges in his red-and-green attempt to dress for success and still fit in with the picnic crowd.

"Crisis, Hal?"

"The Children's Hope League representative is giving a statement to the press. I thought you'd want to be there."

"I do. If you'll both excuse me."

She followed Hal, not unhappy to give Anthony the slip. Somehow their arrival together had lent the situation a proprietary feel, which was completely irrational.

Tess didn't know why her suddenly reawakened hormones were going haywire now, but she wouldn't let them lead her around by the nose. Especially not with a man who hadn't expressed any interest in her beyond what she could do for him.

After allowing Hal to lead her into the crowd, she spent the next hour playing meet and greet with VIPs from the various organizations who'd contributed to her caravan, a charity event to benefit the Children's Hope League.

She liked this organization. They solicited donations all through the year to grant wishes to children suffering from serious illnesses. As a result, today's event required a great deal of schmoozing to get other convention sponsors to donate as generously to the cause.

But despite the hard work, the heat growing steadily more oppressive as the sun climbed in the sky and the fact that her stomach grumbled louder every time someone walked by with food, Tess surveyed the park with a great sense of satisfaction.

She'd coerced the city of New Orleans into lending her decorations from their annual French Quarter Christmas Festival and had recreated the holiday in this park. A twenty-feet-tall tree. Street lamps turned into candy canes dripping with red-and-white garland. Huge plastic poinsettias bordered every walkway.

Even the carnival rides she'd rented reflected the holiday. The moon bounce was red. The giant sack slide was white. The Tilt-A-Whirl blazed red-and-green lights. Santa Clauses and elves milled through the crowds dispensing candy canes, and she'd even hired local singers to spend the day caroling.

In Tess's mind, no Christmas celebration would be complete without gifts, so she'd solicited businesses to load up the tree then invited the local chapter of Big Buddies to attend.

This program paired children with caring mentors, and now big and little buddies milled around, enjoying music, food and fun while awaiting the gift giveaway at the end of the day.

With all the activity and the endless rounds of introductions to keep her busy, Tess couldn't help but notice how Anthony never seemed far from sight. Perhaps it was his height and the blinking antlers, but she picked him out of the crowd no matter where she was. She noticed him giving people a tour of his Firebird then saw him in line at a beverage booth.

Perhaps some sort of hormonal radar had kicked in but when she saw him chatting with the Big Buddies' representative, Tess finally accepted that she simply couldn't ignore the man.

Especially when he stood laughing with a dark-haired woman as if they were two old friends. Tess wondered if they knew each other, *hoped* they did, or he had just lost points for picking up a date during a company function. The man might not be a part of AutoCarTex, but that's exactly what he'd proposed, so she'd hold him to the standard.

Breaking away from a group of conventioneers from Seattle, Tess headed toward the food tent. She needed a meal before her crankiness leaked out all over folks she wanted to impress.

"Not so fast, gorgeous," a male voice called out.

Tess winced at the familiar voice but managed to school her expression by the time she'd turned around to greet the approaching man. "Hello, Daryl. Having a good time today?"

"You look like the perfect Christmas present." He'd dressed in black jeans and a muscle shirt that made him look as bad as his matching Corvette.

"Did you enjoy the tour through town?"

"I would have if I could have seen you around the souped-up Firebird that took my slot."

Tess didn't point out that his vantage was a direct result of his low-riding car. "That was my fault. I insisted on dressing up that Firebird for the parade, so we ran late. The police had to slide us in after the lineup."

"Who's the driver? I saw you talking with him at the speedway yesterday."

"A local business owner."

"Dealer?"

"Service."

A satisfied expression replaced Daryl's frown, and had Tess been a betting woman, she'd have wagered big money that he'd just dismissed Anthony DiLeo as beneath his notice.

"So, Tess, are we on for the rally? We'll have a good time in my 'vette."

"I appreciate the invite, but I told you, Penny flew in specifically to ride with me for the event."

"The rally is supposed to be fun. Not work. Wouldn't you rather make the trip with me?"

No. The upcoming rally was a competitive run over public roads under ordinary traffic rules. For four days, the drivers would head west, stopping at prearranged checkpoints. The thought of being trapped inside the Corvette's tiny interior with Daryl Keene nearly cost her the appetite currently gnawing its way toward her spine.

"I'm sure it would be fun, but—"

"Don't rule it out yet. We've still got a few days. Who knows what will happen. Hal told me Penny had trouble getting away from the office. He said everyone's been working hard on the launch of your new locations."

Hal would never have passed out that information unless Daryl had pressed him, and she suppressed a wave of irritation that this man seemed determined to strong-arm her into a date. "Penny has been working hard. She'll enjoy a break."

He ignored her and peered around her hat, his gaze narrowing. "I haven't heard word one about where we're headed."

"The committee's hush-hush. You know that. Only the car club president has final approval, so no one should know our destination until the start of the race."

"Yeah, but something usually leaks out. I don't think that's all bad, either. It builds the suspense."

Before Tess could reply, she discovered exactly what—or *who* in this case—had put the scowl on Daryl's face.

Anthony DiLeo—carrying a tray of food.

"I brought you something to eat." Extending a hand to Daryl, he introduced himself.

"Daryl Keene."

"The black Corvette."

Daryl only nodded, apparently not needing to ask what Anthony drove after riding the Firebird's bumper through town. Who could miss those antlers?

"Tess said you owned a garage," Daryl said, and the way he said it made it sound like a disease.

"Anthony DiLeo Automotive. New Orleans. You're with Keene Motors out of Tulsa?"

"I'm Keene Motors."

The crown prince of the empire. And while Tess had to admit dealerships in major cities spanning three states made the Keene empire an impressive one, she thought Daryl sounded as though he had something to prove.

Maybe he did. To her mind, Anthony DiLeo's easy pride shone a lot brighter by comparison.

"Well, Keene Motors," Anthony said. "Hate to interrupt, but Tess has been on the run all day. She needs to eat."

That caught *her* off guard. She wasn't sure whether his statement—as if it was any of his business when she ate—or hearing her name in that whiskey-rich voice surprised her most. He made a simple, one-syllable name sound personal.

Too personal, apparently. Testosterone surged between these men so fast she expected it to knock them backward. Had Tess not been so surprised, she might have assumed control quicker, or laughed. Something about these two squaring off in the middle of a park reminded her of bullies sparring during school recess.

Dressed in black, Daryl looked like Billy Badass. And while Anthony DiLeo might look like one of Santa's finest, even the antlers couldn't hide the rugged street-savvy male beneath the casual expression. The man had too much unleashed tension simmering below the surface, visible in an attitude that said, "Want to push? Go on. Try me."

Despite the biceps, Daryl was all polished manners and private schools. The prince of his daddy's domain, defending his turf because he'd decided she was a potential princess.

The kicker—neither of these men was interested in *her*, only in what she could do for *them*. She might not have figured out what Daryl wanted yet, but from the depths of her soul, she knew he wanted more than to get inside her jeans.

Plucking a small tart from a plate, Tess popped it into her mouth. The flaky pastry melted around some heavenly spicy filling. She swallowed and heaved a sigh. "Thanks so much, Anthony. I am starved. So if you gents will excuse me…" She reached for the tray, but Anthony clung to it with a death grip.

"Lead the way." He inclined his blinking antlers toward the picnic table area, making his bells jingle wildly. Then he said to Daryl, "If you'll excuse *us*."

Daryl's scowl said everything—the crown prince didn't like being dismissed by a local garage owner.

"Gentlemen, the only thing I'm interested in right now is food. So if you'll excuse *me*."

Tess wouldn't touch this situation with her daddy's cattle prod. She didn't want to spend time with either man right now, and didn't have to. Not when there was a whole tent nearby filled with food... She didn't wait around to find out what Anthony would do but let her nose lead her away.

The tasty meat pie did nothing but jump-start her appetite, and she groaned when she saw the line leading to the buffet. She debated whether her VIP status would justify a cut to the front when a familiar voice said, "No sense waiting in that line when I've got all this here."

That whiskey voice ruffled through her like a warm breeze, and she spun around to find Anthony, holding up the tray as a peace offering. "Sorry I chased off your friend."

His grin suggested he wasn't sorry at all. Neither was she, for that matter, but she wouldn't tell him.

"You didn't make Daryl *your* friend." She slid onto an empty bench at a nearby picnic table.

"Probably a good thing I didn't come to this convention to make friends."

He'd come to pitch his AutoTexCare plan. She'd gotten that part loud and clear.

Setting down the tray, Anthony sat across from her. Tess ignored him, spread a napkin across her lap and dug in.

"This beats the hell out of hot dogs," he said. "Did you choose the Réveillon feast?"

She nodded, her mouth too occupied with a bite of chicken and oyster gumbo to answer. Divine.

He occupied himself arranging plates then slid the tray out of reach, clearing her path to all the tasty dishes. Looked as if he'd brought her a few bites of everything, and she gave Anthony DiLeo a few points back for thoughtfulness and practicality.

"The restaurant I used to cater suggested the menu," she told him. "Supposedly this is New Orleans's Christmas feast."

"You did good for an out-of-towner. This restaurant actually does justice to the menu."

She resisted another bite and swirled the spoon around the bowl. "Since we're on the subject, what exactly is a Réveillon feast? I was never clear on the point. I think I insulted the restaurant manager when I told him to fax the menu to avoid a blow-by-blow account of how the chef prepared each dish."

Anthony laughed, a rich sound that managed to drag her attention from the gumbo. She could feel his knees pressed close beneath the table. Knew that if he stretched out a hand, their fingers would meet right beside the cake plate.

He was just so…*male*. The thoroughly unnoticeable act of sitting suddenly became noticeable, and her chest constricted enough so breathing required conscious effort.

"Le Réveillon is the awakening," he explained in a smooth-a-hand-over-velvet voice. "It's what families do after midnight mass on Christmas Eve."

"And the chefs around here take their feasts seriously."

"*Chère,* this is New Orleans." He drawled the name into one long word that sounded like N'awlins.

She couldn't help but smile. "I might have heard somewhere that people around here take their food seriously."

"*Very* seriously." He grabbed one of the two bottled

waters and twisted the lid before explaining how Louisiana Cajuns and Creoles inherited the custom from their European ancestors.

His story ended when the representative of the local Big Buddies' chapter showed up.

Anthony made space for her on his bench. "Tess, do you—"

"We've met," she said.

Courtney Gerard shifted a crystal-gray gaze her way. "I know I already thanked you for inviting our chapter to your event, Tess, but let me say it again. This day is turning out to be really great. Every one of the Big Buddies I talked to has told me how much the kids are enjoying themselves. Not only the rides, but they love the cars."

"I'm glad."

Tess shouldn't want to know how these two were acquainted. For all she knew, Anthony serviced Courtney's car. But there was something personal in their body language—this wasn't the first time they'd sat close. "So how do you two know each other?"

"Courtney is my…" He hesitated, frowning down at the beautiful woman. "What exactly are you?"

"I'm like a sister-in-law." She sounded offended he'd even asked. "I don't have a drop of Italian in me, Tess. But once you've been adopted by the DiLeo family, you're family for life. Today I'm Anthony's character reference."

"She's going to tell you how wonderful I am."

Courtney slung her arm around his neck. "This man is *beyond* wonderful. Locals call him Mr. Noble-enough-to-be-a-saint. Kids and dogs follow him wherever he goes. Need I say more?"

Anthony gleamed smug approval, and Tess sank her

spoon back into the bowl. In his fitted jeans and mesh tank that hinted at the golden hairs sprinkling the sculpted chest below, about the last thing to come to mind about this man was sainthood.

But steamy, sweaty sex definitely made the list.

4

THE PICNIC WOUND DOWN late in the day, and Anthony found himself back in the parking lot to show off his car. He'd just said goodbye to a couple from Kenner when he spotted Keene Motors, bypassing his Corvette and heading straight for him.

"Damn," Anthony muttered.

"Why are you getting in my way with Tess?"

As this jerk had been popping up around her all day, Anthony could have asked the same thing. But he refused to get sucked into a pissing contest and shot for diplomacy instead. "She and I have business to discuss."

"Didn't look like business, DiLeo. Looked like lunch."

Anthony circled his car, fitted the key in the trunk lock and tried to look casual. "How does this concern you?"

"I'm interested in her."

"Is she interested in you?"

"We're getting to know each other," he said. "I plan to continue. Take the hint."

That sounded like more of an order than a hint. It turned out to be a winning combination with the guy's attitude, which screamed Anthony should be the one to step aside.

"You dating her?" he asked flatly.

A hard scowl answered that question.

"Then there's no reason why I can't get to know her, too."

"Except that she's out of your league, DiLeo. *Way* out."

Anthony had zero patience for this argument. He might have decided to keep things professional with Tess, but he was just cranky enough about that decision to go head-to-head with this overindulged rich boy. "Maybe that'll work in my favor. Tess doesn't seem too impressed by your league."

The lady herself cut off further reply when she strolled toward them with a group of people. Big Buddies, Anthony guessed, by the mixed ages.

Because of the caravan lineup, she'd parked her Gremlin in the spot beside his, and he had to bite back a smile when Keene Motors scowled even harder. Tess inclined her head in polite greeting as she passed, then entertained her audience with facts about her unique car.

Anthony watched her, and a rush of awareness sucker punched him. She moved around her car with fluid strides, all sleek motion and liquid grace.

He couldn't help but stare when she leaned over to open her door. Those holiday short-shorts left miles of long leg bare. Stylish platform sandals showed off polished red toenails.

It was no wonder he'd had a dream about this woman last night. Sexy babes showcasing high-ticket cars during the months of the year was tradition with car enthusiasts—much like *Sports Illustrated* and their annual swimsuit issue. He'd grown up with those sexy calendars gracing the garage wall, and he'd spent more than his fair share of time sneaking peeks at his favorites whenever his dad and older brothers weren't around.

Tess was the real deal, and while he intended to keep things on the up-and-up with her, he was on fire inside. He hadn't been this attracted to a woman since he'd had his one shot at true love and blown it.

And he'd blown it with Harley big.

It might have taken time, but he'd finally accepted that he wouldn't get a second shot at that kind of love again. No man could be so lucky. He'd had everything in his life, and in his bed, but had been too wrapped up in career ambitions and the thrill of the chase to make it his. As a result, a special woman had gotten away.

He had no one but himself to blame for getting to watch Harley live a head-over-heels love with someone else while he blew through one quick-to-burn, just-as-quick-to-burn-out relationship after another. And with each passing year, even the satisfaction of his career and thrill of the chase wore thinner.

Until now.

He found the idea of chasing Tess a thrill in the extreme. She was hands-down gorgeous, and the combination of her fast answers and Texas twang made his gut clench like a fist.

Unfortunately, he was a day late and a dollar short.

With approximately twenty-four hours before this convention ended, he barely had enough time to prove he was worthy of an introduction to her father, let alone a date after they concluded their business.

And then there was a significant logistical problem. Louisiana and Texas might share a border, but he couldn't easily show up on her doorstep in Lubbock with an invite for dinner.

Before he had the chance to consider that, Anthony

found himself jerked from his thoughts by the sight of a familiar face in the crowd. He didn't know this man personally, but after a lifetime spent around cars, he couldn't have missed him.

Number 7. The Maverick.

Everyone even remotely interested in racing, and likely many who weren't, had heard of Ray Macy, a racing legend. Anthony had more than a passing interest and had seen the Maverick race numerous times on New Orleans's very speedway. A big cowboy wearing hand-tooled boots and a flashy silver belt buckle, he was as large in person as he was on TV.

Anthony watched with growing amazement as he cut a path through the cars straight toward them.

Tess was just saying goodbye to her group and glanced up with a look of pleased surprise. "Hey, hey, Uncle Ray."

"Hello, sweet thing." The Maverick scooped her into his arms for a hug.

Anthony claimed to have done his homework, but he'd obviously fallen short on the job. He'd had no clue Ray Macy was Tess's uncle. Suddenly her skill on the racetrack made sense.

He wasn't about to let this opportunity pass, so when Ray Macy let his niece go, Anthony moved toward them and extended his hand. "Anthony DiLeo, sir. Pleased to meet you."

The man shook with a firm grip, looking unsure why he should be interested.

"Anthony is the owner of a local service center, Uncle Ray. We've been discussing service in this market."

This wasn't exactly the truth, but it was enough of a connection to Tess and AutoCarTex to spark Ray Macy's interest.

"Pleased to meet you, Anthony. We're putting a lot of emphasis on our expansion into Louisiana."

"I didn't realize you were affiliated with AutoCarTex."

"Technically, he's not," Tess explained. "He's Daddy's right-hand man."

"And sweet thing's, too." Ray shot her a fond smile.

Which would explain why Anthony hadn't come across the man's name during his research.

"So what are you doing here, Uncle Ray?"

"I've come to swap places with Penny."

One glimpse at Tess and Anthony knew this wasn't news she wanted to hear.

Obviously Uncle Ray recognized the same thing because he held up his hands and said, "Now before you start bucking, let me tell you that I already promised your daddy."

"There's no need for this." She sounded exasperated. "If Penny has to head back to Lubbock, fine. I'll drive the rally on my own. I never invited her in the first place."

"Your daddy wants to sleep at night."

Anthony grasped an idea of what was happening here. Tess had said she was scheduled to drive in the rally tomorrow and it looked as if her driving buddy had a sudden change of plans.

He didn't understand why Tess's father wouldn't sleep at night if she drove alone but couldn't think of a way to ask without sounding as though he was butting into family business.

"I disagree." Keene Motors strolled toward them. "Hey, Ray. Good to see you again. My father mentioned something about threatening letters. He said Big Tex is worried about Tess."

Judging by her narrowing gaze, this wasn't anything Tess wanted to hear, either. "Daddy's gotten letters before."

"What letters?" Anthony seized his opportunity.

Tess waved a dismissive hand. "With the TV promotional campaign, Daddy gets lots of viewer mail. Not all of it good."

"He's gotten some correspondence lately that has him worried," Ray Macy said, "Rightfully so, in my opinion. Especially after the one that arrived yesterday."

"My father told me these letters mention family members." Keene Motors looked appropriately concerned for the occasion, but Anthony couldn't shake the feeling that he was pleased with himself for having inside information.

"What did this one say?" Tess asked, looking worried.

"This one took your daddy down for the TV ads. Said he should stop trying to be everybody's friend and pay more attention to his daughter." Ray Macy slipped his arm around her and gave a fond squeeze. "Now you see why he doesn't want you on the road alone, sweet thing?"

"I do understand, but I thought you were putting your new car in the Phoenix 1000. You said you were pressed getting her ready. You can't take time to drive the rally with me."

"Of course I can. Anything for my favorite niece."

"I'm your only niece."

"If you don't want to rally with your uncle, Tess, my offer still stands," Keene Motors said. "Drive with me."

Did Keene Motors really think he could bully Tess? He might be *getting to know* her, but he obviously didn't know enough yet. Anthony had only been around a few days, but he already understood that this woman did not like to be pushed.

Uncle Ray didn't say a word. Neither did Anthony. He held his breath instead, waiting to see which way Tess went.

"I appreciate the offer, Daryl," she said. "But I'm thinking it might be smarter to use the time to work."

Keene Motors looked irritated. "You'll back out *now?*"

"I said *work.*" She narrowed her gaze. "Anthony and I are in the middle of discussing some business. He offered to drive the rally with me, but I turned him down because Penny was here."

Anthony saw right through her attempt to use him to sidestep this situation, and since Tess had just given him the mother of all chances to impress her, he'd damn sure make good.

"Obviously I understood that Tess had previous plans," he said. "So I offered to make a trip to Lubbock. But driving the rally together would give us the time we need to cover all our business a lot sooner—"

"And save you the trouble of the drive, Uncle Ray."

"What business?" Keene Motors demanded, drawing all their surprised gazes.

"Business between Anthony and me," Tess said coolly.

Keene Motors shot Ray a disbelieving look. "I don't like this one bit, Ray. We don't know a damn thing about this guy."

Silence fell as hard as the humidity in a New Orleans summer. Keene Motors' comment hit home, and Anthony could see the effect. Ray Macy grew worried. Tess and Keene Motors looked outraged, although likely for different reasons.

"I appreciate your concern, Daryl," Tess said with effort. "But I don't need a babysitter. And I really don't need you telling me how to do my job."

"If it's any help—" Anthony addressed Ray Macy, hoping to smooth through the tense moment "—Tess has been working with my sister-in-law for this convention. My older brother is a lieutenant with the NOPD, and I'm a well-established business owner in this town. You have my word I'll keep her safe."

Ray Macy still looked dubious, and Tess must have realized that, because she sidled close enough to raise a question about whether their business might be mixed with pleasure.

Linking her arm through his, she gazed up at him, her green eyes sparkling with challenge. "Anthony's trustworthy, Uncle Ray, and he's been dying for a ride in my Gremlin."

ANTHONY DILEO switched gears so fast that even Tess was impressed. He didn't blink when she dragged him into the fray, and smoothly assumed control of the situation.

"I can't say I've been *dying* for a ride in her car," he told Uncle Ray, "but I am looking forward to it."

"How long have you known my niece?"

Uh-oh. "Do you want Anthony to sign something in blood to take back to Daddy?"

"You're all chuckles today, sweet thing." In a lightning-fast move, he had his Stetson off his head and on hers, flipping the brim down so she couldn't see. "I don't need blood, but your new friend here has to be clear that if anything happens to you, he'll be answering to me."

"I understand, sir," Anthony said, very respectfully. "My intentions toward your niece are honorable."

Tess flipped the hat from her head and shot him a look. *Honorable?* She'd see how *honorable* he'd still be when they were alone. She had a hankering to pull out that rebellious ponytail and see what that tawny hair looked like after she'd run her fingers through it.

"I'll keep my cell phone on, so you can check in with me whenever you feel the need, Uncle Ray. Tell Daddy."

"You tell him yourself."

She should have known she'd get no help on this. Not with the way Daryl had gotten his hackles up about Anthony.

"I'll give you my cell number just in case." Anthony whipped his wallet from a back pocket and withdrew a business card before wandering off to his car for a pen.

He jotted down a few numbers, and she watched Uncle Ray put on his imposing look, a surprisingly grim face for a normally good-natured man.

Anthony handed him the card. "My service center number is on the front and my home and cell numbers are on the back. I also wrote down my brother Nic's number at the police station. Call anytime. The duty sergeant can always get through to him. And this—" he pointed to the bottom of the card "—is my mother's number. Call her anytime, too. She's someone else I'll be answering to if I don't take good care of your niece."

Tess burst out laughing, and Uncle Ray's frown melted in a look that suggested he appreciated not only the numbers but the humor. Good for Anthony.

Daryl looked incredulous. "You're going to check this guy out, Ray, aren't you?"

Not that it was any of his business, Tess thought, folding her arms across her chest. "You're kidding, right?"

"The rally doesn't start until tomorrow," Uncle Ray said. "I'll have your daddy run the drill."

"The drill?" Anthony asked.

"The drill." She rolled her eyes. "If a guy smiles and says hello, Daddy has his security chief run a background check."

"By the way, sweet thing, I'll be bunking with you tonight. There's not a room to be had at the Chase."

The way Uncle Ray was eyeing Anthony, he probably wanted to make sure she didn't get too close to the man before he saw the results of that background check.

She had plans for Anthony DiLeo all right, but they'd wait until they were on the road and well away from her babysitters.

"So, is everyone finally satisfied with my plans for the rally?" she asked, earning a curious glance from Anthony who clearly hadn't missed her sarcasm.

"Good to see you again, Ray." Daryl extended his hand then stalked off with barely a nod.

He ignored Anthony completely.

Withdrawing her hotel key card from the convention badge she wore around her neck, she handed it to her uncle. "I won't be leaving here for a while yet, so you can get settled in."

"Trying to get rid of me?"

She leaned up on tiptoe and kissed his cheek. "Yes."

He laughed. "What's on the agenda tonight?"

Tess invited him to join her for the awards banquet, and he agreed to come—so he wouldn't miss a chance to interrogate Anthony, no doubt. She saw him off to the hotel, and when she returned to her car, she found Anthony waiting.

"Am I a convenient escape from your overprotective family?"

"Would it bother you if you were?"

"A little."

"Yet you're willing to come anyway. Even if it means driving in my Gremlin." She eyed him curiously. "So you're willing to get involved with me to get your introduction?"

"No, Tess, I'm not." His gaze flashed golden fire. "I won't try to manipulate you. That's not how I operate."

"Glad to hear it." Not that she thought he *could* manipulate her. She'd cut her teeth on men who were a lot less noble and straightforward than this one.

"Then, Anthony, the answer to your question is yes and no. Yes, I used you to sidestep my babysitters and, no, that wasn't the only reason. I'd like to spend some time alone with you."

That fire in his eyes flared hotter now, not indignation but desire, a look that made the bottom of her stomach swoop wildly like a ride on the back of a bucking bronco.

But she sobered up quick enough when she caught Daryl watching them from his car. She didn't like the look on his face one bit. Anthony hadn't made him a friend, and now she'd publicly rejected him on top of it.

Then again, who was Daryl to use her uncle's concern to strong-arm her into driving the rally together? She'd been polite, but clear she wasn't interested. Just as she'd been polite but clear when rebuffing every one of his advances.

The man refused to let her off the hook. Still, in hindsight, she shouldn't have let her irritation get the better of her. There were much more effective ways to handle someone like Daryl. Flaunting another man in his face wasn't one.

"Here's the deal," she said, eager to cut to the chase. "How about four days on the open road. You, me. No babysitters. No strings. Just some fun. What do you say?"

He didn't answer right away. Tess knew he wanted her—she hadn't misread those signals—but something was holding him back, and that surprised her.

"What is it?"

He reached up and suddenly his thumb glanced the length of her jaw, a whisper-soft touch of calloused skin that galvanized her to the spot. It took a moment to realize he'd only brushed away a strand of hair.

"I was hell-bent on staying professional." A soft smile touched his lips, lips that were just perfect for kissing. "I didn't want to get business tangled up with personal."

"Oh, well." She flipped her hair back haughtily and spun on her heels. "If your introduction to my daddy is more important than having fun with me then your loss."

He snagged his arm around her waist, stopping her short so suddenly she let out a gasp.

"That's not what I said, Tess." He steadied her against him, his face pressed close to hers. "I'm willing to give up my business with your father for a chance to know you."

His words got lost somewhere in her hair, a promise that filtered through her like a warm caress.

Well, that was more along the lines of what she'd been looking for. "Lucky for you, business and pleasure aren't mutually exclusive. Why don't we agree to keep them separate? It'll be a nice break from reality, don't you think?"

"Providing my background check meets with approval."

Tess laughed. "There is that, of course."

But she knew by the heat in his eyes that they were going to have a good time on the open road and *honorable* would only play a small part.

5

HAD IT ONLY BEEN a few days since he'd arrived in the hotel looking for a lady named Tess? In his wildest dreams, Anthony couldn't have imagined what he'd find.

The lady in question had dressed for comfortable driving in a yellow T-shirt and shorts that hinted at all her inviting curves. Her sleek legs drew his gaze down to the strappy slide-ons that left her toes bare.

"You, me. No babysitters. No strings. Just some fun. What do you say?"

Anthony said he wouldn't have missed this trip for anything. He wanted more time with Tess—not only to prove he was worth that introduction to her father, but so he could figure out exactly what was happening between them.

Whatever it was, it felt good.

He watched her maneuver through the Sunday-morning traffic, which would have been light but for the jam of classic cars now crowding I-10's lanes. Thirty-seven rally contestants had left the hotel to fanfare from the conventioneers, and the excitement continued well beyond the speedway.

He extended his arm out the open window and waved yet again when a motorist honked and raced to keep up with them. "Is this going to happen all the way to San Francisco?"

"It won't be so bad once we get underway and the drivers head off on their own routes. Right now we look like a parade."

They were surrounded on all sides by mint-condition classics, ranging from those with their original parts to ones like Tess's that had been souped up into impressive-looking hot rods. "Damn straight."

She smiled, the morning sun washing her profile in light. She looked excited to be on the road, even a little breathless.

He leaned back in the seat, contented by a physical awareness he hadn't felt in so long he'd forgotten the feeling. "Explain to me how this parade is supposed to be a race. I missed that part at the send-off this morning."

The car club had sponsored a farewell breakfast where the rally contestants received their travel instructions in a ceremony that combined sealed envelopes and a video presentation to rival the Academy Awards.

"It's more of a symbolic race," she said. "We don't put our foot to the floor and make a straight run. We drive our own routes, stopping at checkpoints every night."

"With our checkpoints in Dallas, Santa Fe and Las Vegas it won't be hard to come up with alternate highways."

"That's the point. It's no fun if everyone travels the same roads. We all pick what we think will be the most interesting route and bring in a souvenir when we pit stop at night."

"So whoever makes the checkpoint first each night wins?"

She shook her head, sending glossy waves tumbling around her shoulders in a sexy spill that made him think of what she'd look like wearing nothing but that hair and a smile. "We compare rankings, but there are no winners in the conventional sense. Except for the Women's Cancer League, of course. Earning money for them is the whole point. Whoever ranks first on the final day will have the privilege of presenting the check to the Cancer League representative."

Anthony still didn't get the *race* part, but he wasn't about to complain.

"Trust me, Anthony. You're in for a treat," she said. "The rally committee does something special at each checkpoint to pamper us after a long day on the road. We'll get a good bit of promotion for our businesses, too. But most importantly, we just want to have a good time."

She seemed so focused on having fun that he could only guess that she'd been as bored with life as he'd been lately. Not so surprising given the protective people in her life.

"Y'know, Tess, I told you I'd done my research, but I had no idea you were related to Ray Macy. I suppose I should have figured something was up with the way you drive."

"I'll take that as a compliment."

"It is."

"There's no reason you should have known about Uncle Ray. He's not technically with AutoCarTex, even if he does do more work for Daddy than the VIPs."

"He's your mother's brother?"

She nodded, shifting her gaze up to the rearview mirror for a quick peek. "Her older and *only* brother."

"I can't speak to the only part, but as an older brother, I can understand why he'd be so protective of his niece."

She grimaced. "When he's not worrying about me, he's worrying about my daddy."

"When does he find the time? He races hard. I follow his career."

"Daddy and I are his only family. He never married, so he takes his wonderful nurturing soul and points it our way. He promised my mom before she died that he'd look after us the same way he looked after her. He's never stopped."

"When did you lose your mom?"

She smiled softly. "A long time ago. I was ten."

"Accident?"

"Cancer."

"That's rough."

She only inclined her head, but knowing Big Tex had reared his only daughter with his brother-in-law's help fitted another piece into the puzzle about this woman.

"I lost my father when I was eight," he said, sharing the sense of loss that years didn't diminish. "A massive heart attack. It happened so fast I always wished we'd had a warning, some more time before he died."

"I'm sorry for you and your family. There were some good things about knowing my mom was dying. We got to blow off the rest of life and make the most of the time we had left together. We said things we might not have said if we hadn't known we wouldn't get another chance." Tess shook her head, a tiny gesture that convinced Anthony no matter how much time had passed, some memories still hurt. "But she got so sick. It would have been easier on her if she'd gone quicker."

"Losing a parent sucks no matter what."

"Yeah." The conversation faded off into a thoughtful silence, broken only by the steady hum of the engine and the miles rolling under their tires.

"Are you sorry you brought the subject up?" she asked.

"Just sorry I made you sad."

"Memories are a part of who I am." She shifted her gaze off the road and gave him a smile. "I assume that's what this is all about. You want to know about me."

"I do." He fingered a soft brown curl that trailed along the back of the seat. "Don't you want to know about me?"

"It'll be a long couple of days if we don't talk."

"That's the truth."

She didn't seem to mind the intimacy of him touching her hair, so he thumbed the sleek texture, liked the connection between them, no matter how small.

"So your father never remarried?"

"Nope. What about your mom?"

"Nope. She just works a lot and dotes on all of us."

"Sounds exactly like my daddy. He's got AutoCarTex, and he's got me. Toss Uncle Ray into the mix, and I've got two doting men with nothing better to do than mother-hen me."

"I hear a *to death* in there." He tugged the curl just enough so she could feel it, smiled when he noticed the color rise in her cheeks.

"You got that right."

And he did. The tiny frown riding between her brows told him this gorgeous woman risked drowning in good intentions. And while Anthony's pride might have stung that she'd used him to sidestep a babysitter on this trip, he wouldn't have missed this chance to explore this chemistry happening between them.

"I'm glad your father and uncle were satisfied with their background check," he said. "We'll have fun this week."

"I'm counting on it." Shifting her gaze off the road, she glanced over the rims of her stylish sunglasses in a sultry look that made his blood throb hard, and Anthony recognized what he saw in her face.

She was chafing against the restraints of her life.

He knew because Tess wasn't the first woman he'd known to feel this way. There was another woman near and dear to his heart who'd felt smothered beneath the love and concern of her five older brothers.

His baby sister, Frankie.

She'd needed to spread her wings so much that she'd taken off from New Orleans without a backward glance. Except for Christmas and birthday gifts to their mother, not a one of the DiLeo family had heard from her since the day she'd left town.

There was no missing those symptoms in Tess, and Anthony decided right then and there that he wasn't going to make that mistake with her. He met her gaze with a smile and thought…*Tess Hardaway, get ready for the ride of your life.*

TESS SHOULD HAVE BEEN exhausted after a long day on the road. She wouldn't have traded her Gremlin for the world, but even she admitted the ride left a lot to be desired. Late model cars took the miles with smooth aerodynamics, not to mention important amenities like body-hugging seats.

Still, excitement started her pulse speeding as Anthony maneuvered her car through the outskirts of Dallas. Her mood had nothing to do with physical exhaustion and everything to do with physical awareness. A day spent in close quarters with this laughing, handsome man had definitely taken its toll.

And her libido needed no herbal supplements, thanks.

Things hadn't been so bad when she'd been behind the wheel, but sitting in the passenger's seat with nothing to do but notice things about him proved sheer torture.

Mile after mile of that fast smile and deep-throated laugh. Broad, broad shoulders that took up more space than his due. Long fingers poised easily on her steering wheel. That nubby ponytail teasing the headrest of the driver's seat.

Although Tess guessed he'd rather drive than *be* driven, she hadn't had to fight for equal time. They'd made the trip north through Louisiana at a decent clip, stopping every few hours to walk and switch places, making up for those stops by opting for a drive-through lunch.

They'd discussed everything from family to careers, and he'd entertained her with stories from his service center—a huge establishment with employees that sounded like the comedians from *Whose Line Is It Anyway?*

She'd told him about her office inside AutoCarTex Corporate. Not nearly as slapstick as Anthony DiLeo Automotive, perhaps, but she was proud of her work in public relations, liked supporting Daddy's business by spreading around his goodwill.

Not once did Tess feel as if she was getting the third degree. She was, of course, but he'd been so easy to talk to she'd almost forgotten.

They'd even had their first argument about what souvenir from their trip to bring to the checkpoint. But Anthony had managed to be witty and charming, and when he wheeled into the parking lot of the Grand Vista Hotel, she felt a crazy mixture of regret to see the day end and excitement for the night ahead.

"We made it." Slipping the car into gear, he paused with his hand over the ignition. "I know you want to gas up tonight so we can start fresh in the morning, but do you mind if we wait until after check-in? I want to look under the hood to see how she's burning oil."

"Do you think there's a problem?"

"No, this long haul is probably the best thing in the world for her engine, but these old gals need extra special care. I want to get a read on how she's running, and I can't do that until she cools off."

Made sense to Tess. "The sooner we check in the better. Just bring our souvenir. We won't need our luggage yet."

Anthony grimaced, reminding her exactly what he thought about their souvenir—*she'd* won that argument. But he didn't say a word while getting out. "I'll get your door."

Tess reached for her purse and waited as he circled the car, amused by the gesture when she could have been halfway across the parking lot already. But she knew he wanted to impress her. So far he hadn't missed a trick.

The rally committee had set up a banquet room as a pit stop for the contestants, with food and refreshments and a map to chart the day's miles. They bypassed the hotel's front desk and followed signs through the lobby to a marquis that read Rambling Rally Pit Stop.

Anthony sidled around her and grabbed this door, too, and they stepped inside a room that had been decorated with a flashy racetrack theme. Pennants hung from the ceilings bearing names of popular racers. She caught sight of her uncle's and smiled. A buffet and a beverage bar had been set up, and the servers wore coveralls that made them look like part of a pit crew.

"Wow," Anthony said at her side.

"Gotta love this car club. When they host an event, they host it right."

"They? *You.* You're a board member."

"But I'm not on the rally committee." Tess gazed up at him, struck by the sight of him from this vantage point. She'd gotten used to seeing him in profile with his stylish sunglasses shielding those potent dark eyes.

Now he gazed down at her with an amused expression, and she was treated to the full force of his smile—the flash of white teeth, the creases around his mouth that made one smile spread across his whole face.

He was new enough in her life that she wasn't familiar with his striking looks yet. Definitely hadn't grown accustomed to this crazy flutter whenever she glanced his way and found herself surprised by how handsome he was, by her reaction to the chemistry between them.

She had to consciously draw another breath, so she didn't get dizzy.

"Just getting in now, Tess?" a familiar voice asked, stealing away the moment and jerking her back to reality. "Decided to work instead of compete?"

She and Anthony turned in unison to find Daryl sitting at a nearby table with a blonde. Since they'd just walked through the door and were still carrying a souvenir bag, she thought the answer should have been obvious.

"Good drive today?" she asked politely.

"Never better." Daryl shot his companion a cheesy smile

that made her giggle. "Glad you made it safe. But keep my cell number handy in case something comes up. I'd hate to think of you stranded on the open road."

"Daryl—"

"Appreciate the concern." Anthony cut her off. "You don't need to worry about Tess. She's in good hands."

The innuendo in *that* statement wiped the smile from Daryl's face fast, but Anthony didn't give him a chance to reply before leading her to the check-in table.

"Hello, pretty lady." Ralph, the round-cheeked cochair of the rally committee, stood and leaned across the table to kiss her. "Good run today?"

She nodded. "Where are we?"

"Twelfth in the lineup."

"Twelfth? Ugh."

"That's not too shabby, Tess. Twenty-five contestants still haven't made it in yet." Anthony grabbed the clipboard and signed his name before handing it to her.

"True, true," Ralph agreed. "The first day always starts a little slow. You know that."

"True, true." And she was surprised to realize that she protested more out of habit than anything else. She'd enjoyed the ride today, and her companion.

Anthony introduced himself and asked, "So what's next? Souvenirs?"

He held up the bag containing the book of folklore from Melrose Plantation, a Louisiana property whose history revolved around two liberated-before-their-time women. He'd wanted a model of a 1913 steam locomotive, complete with coal car and caboose, from the DeQuincy Railroad Museum. She'd insisted and, after a valiant fight, he'd given in.

To impress her, no doubt.

"Over there." Ralph pointed to a table setup where the few odd packages sat. "But, Tess, before you go, we've got to talk."

"What's up?"

"The hotel messed up the room block."

"You're kidding?"

"It's not tragic, but it isn't good. We're shuffling all the rally committee members around. Tripling up so we can give our rooms to our contestants. We were wondering if you'd stay with Margaret and Janie. Your friend can stay in my room."

Now that wasn't at all what she'd had in mind for her first night on the road with Anthony. And one look at him assured her a slumber party wasn't on his mind, either. "Why don't we just get rooms in the overflow hotel?"

Ralph shook his head and did the closest thing to a scowl that Tess could imagine on a jolly-cheeked man. "No good. The political convention is in town this week along with those makeup ladies who wear the pink jackets. Did you know there are so many of them that their annual conference runs for four weeks? I had *nine* on my plane from New Orleans this morning."

Now it was her turn to frown. "This is Dallas, Ralph. There have got to be rooms somewhere."

"Let me know if you find them. We've been making calls all day. Five would wrap things up nicely."

As a car club board member, Tess couldn't exactly refuse to give up her room while the rest of the committee did. And even if they could find a room elsewhere, she'd look like a problem child by not cooperating, which would reflect poorly on AutoCarTex.

She shot an appealing glance at Anthony, who only nodded. "No problem, Ralph. We'll do our bit for the cause."

"Thanks, Tess. Now go mark today's route on the map. And make sure you eat." He cast a longing glance at the plate piled high at his elbow. "At least they got the barbecue right."

Tess managed a smile. "I won't ask who picked the menu."

"Not impressed, hmm?" Anthony asked as he led her across the room to the map.

"I'm from Lubbock, remember? You sure you're okay with our change of plans?"

"We'll make do. Besides, we've still got some time before we have to hit the sack."

"Are you being *honorable?*"

"Trying."

She chuckled.

"Should I be surprised they assigned us purple?" Anthony asked dryly when they reached the map.

"My car is legend wherever I go."

Reaching for a nearby basket, he began picking out tiny purple pushpins. "Here you go. Start marking."

Tess traced their route off I-10 and noticed that so far they'd been the only ones to travel these roads through Louisiana. "We'll have to look at the maps before splitting up tonight. We have to declare tomorrow's route with the rally committee before we leave in the morning."

"The rally committee knows our route but the other drivers don't, is that it?"

"Right. Liability issue. The committee needs to know which way we're headed in case we have a problem. At night we mark our routes to see how we matched up against everyone else." She frowned at the purple pushpins dotting the map. "We didn't do so hot today. I thought you said this would be the best route off the main highway."

"Depends on your interpretation of *best*. You said you wanted the most interesting, not the quickest."

She huffed. "I've never had such a poor showing, even on the first day of a rally."

Anthony dropped another few pushpins into her palm. "Got more than your fair share of the Maverick's competitive blood, hmm? What was all that you said about getting off the highway to see the countryside and have fun?"

"It's fun to compete even if we can't win. After the way you beat me at the speedway, I shouldn't need to explain that."

"You want to have fun, see the sights and rank number one, too. So you basically want everything."

"Is that really so much for a girl to ask?"

"Not with me, it's not." He shot her a totally roguish look, and Tess laughed, drawing the attention of several folks around them. Including Daryl, who narrowed his gaze.

"You are such a bad influence."

"Me, *chère?*" That roguish grin faded into a look of pure innocence. "What makes you say that?"

"Oh, please. Let's get out of here."

"No barbecue? Don't tell me you're not hungry." Now it was Anthony shooting the longing look at Ralph's buffet.

"I don't want to eat here."

She didn't have to say another word. Anthony led her out of the room and even went so far as to get directions to a Chinese place within walking distance. It wasn't long until they were back at the hotel, strolling a path around a lake, discussing tomorrow's route and munching from a meal in cardboard boxes.

"You seem awfully familiar with takeout," she said.

"I'm a healthy boy, and since I don't live at home…"

"Actually, I'm very impressed." She speared her chopsticks into her chow mein. "This was a great idea. I was dreading the thought of getting back into the car again."

"Just stick with me, and you can have it all."

She chuckled, and the sound faded in the twilight as they walked along, enjoying their meal in the golden spill of light from the lamps that marked the path and the black lake.

There was nothing like the Texas sky at sunset. The sky was bigger, the colors sharper and when darkness finally fell, it fell with a weight that seemed to cloak the whole world.

"So what's bugging you about Keene Motors?" Anthony asked.

Tess swallowed hastily and glanced at him in surprise. "Where did that come from?"

"You were willing to get back in the car just to get away from him. I didn't for a minute believe it was the barbecue. You're from Lubbock, remember?"

"Okay, it wasn't the barbecue," she admitted.

"Jealous?"

That made her laugh. "Hardly. Appreciative is more like it. That blonde seemed pretty caught up in him. I'm hoping this means he's found someone new to stalk."

"Harsh."

"Maybe, but he really had no right to be rude to you. We never dated, and I certainly never strung him along."

"He was trying to make himself feel better at my expense."

"That didn't bother you?"

He grimaced. "Of course it bothered me. But I'm all about what's going to impress you, which left me to choose between demonstrating my awesome self-restraint or letting Keene Motors drag me into a pissing contest."

"Point taken."

Loud and clear. A reminder of the reason Anthony wanted to impress her should have been enough to knock the edge off this feeling that they were the only two people on the planet.

It didn't. She was so aware of him, from his long-legged strides to the fingers maneuvering chopsticks in his carton. "I suppose I shouldn't be surprised after the way I handled him. I should have demonstrated as much self-restraint."

"Listen, Tess, I don't know what's been happening between you two before this convention, but I will say I'm not impressed with what I've seen. He should have backed off when you turned down his invitation to drive the rally. Using your uncle to try and get his way wasn't right."

"I only challenged him, and he was challenged enough."

Anthony stabbed his chopsticks inside his carton. He wrapped an arm around Tess's shoulder, a gesture that smacked more of reassurance than it did intimacy. But the instant her body came up against his, every nerve felt as though it suddenly ignited.

He possessed the kind of wiry strength that came from more than just working out. He lived a physically active life and she found his strength very appealing.

"Don't worry, *chère.* Keene Motors wasn't going to

like anyone who came near you. And while you might have made him unhappy, you made me *very* happy."

"You're making fun of me."

"I'd never make fun of you. If Keene Motors doesn't want to get burned, he shouldn't play with matches."

"Meaning I'm combustible?"

He squeezed her playfully. "Meaning the idiot shouldn't try to bully anyone unless he's willing to deal with the consequences. If the guy's been refusing to take *no* for an answer, you were within your rights to put him in his place. And witnesses never hurt. Especially when they're men who'll jump all over a chance to defend you."

She laughed, unable to help herself. No matter what Anthony said, Tess could have handled the situation with Daryl better, but he was very gallant to make excuses for her. And his excuses did make her feel better.

His nearness, too. He kept his arm around her as they walked back to the hotel, a sweet gesture that made her smile into the darkness. Penny was right—she hadn't been making enough time to have fun lately. One day of laughter drove home just how long it had been since she'd felt like laughing.

But between Daddy's letters and Daryl's hot pursuit, it was no wonder Tess had taken refuge in work. Yet now she had Anthony. For a few days at least. While she regretted that they'd lose tonight, she made the most of the moment by ogling his tight butt when he headed under her hood to check her fluids. Then she went a step further by snuggling close to him when he carried her garment bag upstairs to her room.

Tess's roommates were already there. Margaret and Janie were both nearing retirement age and owned different models of classic Mustangs, but that was where their similarities ended. Margaret was a grandmother who'd decided the garden club just wasn't her speed while Janie, who'd never married, had enjoyed the jet-setting life of a wealthy eccentric.

A car club event didn't go by without her sharing some story about a former lover from somewhere around the globe. This time it had been Ernst, who'd been of imperial Hapsburg descent and who had sequestered her inside an Austrian hotel room and made her miss an entire month-long tour of the Alps.

Janie watched Anthony appreciatively as he crossed the room to hang the garment bag in the closet, and Tess had to bite back a smile when he turned around, looking oblivious to the little old lady who was eyeing him as though he was a before-bed mint.

His gaze didn't miss the bed, though, and Tess's smile faded fast. Since deciding to proposition this man, she had to share her sleeping arrangements with Uncle Ray and now this duo of white-haired hot mamas. Things weren't going along anything like the way she'd intended.

But she did appreciate Anthony's ability to go with the flow. No doubt Daryl would have seen that bed as the land of opportunity and not gone down without a fight. Not Anthony, who just rolled with the punches, which had made things so much easier on everyone.

Leaning back against her door, Tess adopted a nicely casual pose, tipping her head back just enough to make her hair slither behind her shoulders. A kissing-perfect pose.

"Thanks, Anthony." She dropped her voice a throaty octave.

"My pleasure, Tess."

He pulled up in front of her, so close she could feel the heat radiating off his big body. He gazed down into her face, his expression just as warm, and the breath locked tight in her chest as she forgot everything but the sight of this oh-so-handsome man staring down at her with such longing in his eyes.

The moment was powerful. Even with Margaret and Janie watching. Awareness was all over him, a physical thing, and Tess stood there, lips parted, wanting a kiss more than she could ever remember wanting a kiss before.

For the space of a heartbeat, she saw arousal flare in his eyes then he lowered his face to hers and brushed that kissing mouth across her lips, the prelude to a real kiss, a promise.

"Sleep well, Tess, ladies." Then he disappeared into the hallway, and she stared after him, exhaling a sigh that made Margaret and Janie laugh.

6

ANTHONY YAWNED, unable to stop himself.

"You don't look like you slept much last night," Tess said. "Want me to pull over for coffee at the next Starbucks?"

"I spent the night imagining what you looked like in bed," he admitted.

She only laughed, and somehow it seemed preordained that he wouldn't get much sleep around her. Had it not been for her roommates, he'd never have been able to stop with one polite kiss. Not with his head filled with the memory of his sexy dream and the taste of her sweet lips. Not with his body honed to a fine edge after a day of driving together in close quarters. Not when he'd just walked through the starry Texas night with his arm wrapped around her, feeling as if she belonged tucked up against him, all warm and soft and sexy.

So he'd taken a cold shower then lain awake all night, thinking about Tess in the next room, imagining her stripping off the shorts outfit that had started the day so fresh and feminine and had ended no less attractive for the wrinkles.

He imagined her in the shower with her creamy skin all sleek and soapy beneath running water and scented lather.

He imagined what she would feel like naked against him, spread out under the covers, her long legs twined through his.

"Coffee isn't a bad idea," he said. "I need to get my blood flowing."

"Really?"

That statement dripped with innuendo, and before he had a clue what she was about, she'd swung the steering wheel a hard right. Gravel kicked up under the tires in a fierce complaint as she rode along the shoulder.

"Tess, what the hell—"

He cut off short as the car jerked to a stop and he grabbed the dash to brace himself. Dirt billowed up around the windows as she slammed the car into Park hard enough to make the steering column rattle.

"Kiss me, Anthony. Just kiss me."

He didn't get a chance to reply before she reached out, slipped her fingers into his hair and pulled him toward her.

Anthony had known from the second he'd met Tess that if he let go, he'd never be able to stop kissing her.

He let go.

His mouth came down on hers hard, and she made a small sound as her lips parted, all yielding softness and insistent need. The moment ground to a stop, and the world outside of the Gremlin fell away as if it never existed. The whiz of cars speeding past faded into the distance.

All Anthony could hear was their breaths colliding in greedy appreciation. He hadn't been the only one aching. He tasted Tess's impatience, an erotic mingling of sense and touch as her tongue swept boldly inside his mouth, another challenge, and every nerve ending in his body gathered in reply, so sharply in tune with this woman that he grabbed her to hang on.

His hands threaded around her neck, her soft skin yielding as she let him pull her deeper into their kiss. He inhaled the sultry vanilla-almond scent of her hair, tasted the coffee still lingering in her sweet mouth.

His body felt as if it had been honed in on a special frequency, and he could only think about the way she tasted, the way her skin felt beneath his fingers, the way her mouth demanded a response. And got one.

His whole body ached with a slow, potent burn. He wanted to drag her into his lap and wrap himself around her, test this sensation everywhere his naked skin could touch her naked skin.

But she was trapped behind the wheel, straining toward him, and he could only use his hands to explore, only make love to her mouth, only marvel at how she made love to his mouth back.

And it wasn't until a shrill horn screeched as a car sped past that they finally sprang apart.

A minute later or a day, Anthony couldn't say. He could only stare at the sight she made with her chocolate hair ruffled around her face, her cheeks flushed and green eyes alive with pleasure, and amusement.

"Blood flowing yet?"

He shook his head to clear it. "Damn."

She laughed, a silvery, satisfied sound, and he could only stare across the distance, at those kiss-swollen lips.

"I knew I'd like kissing you."

And right then Anthony knew a need for this woman that transcended the physical ache pulling at every part of him, making him fight the urge to drag her back into his arms and lose himself inside this incredible heat they made together.

"I wanted to kiss you like that last night," she said.

God, what was it about hearing this woman admit she wanted him that struck a blow that almost felt physical?

Unable to resist, he reached up, dragged his thumb along her cheek. "Just wait until tonight, Tess. Just wait."

Threading his fingers along her jaw, he tilted her face up for another kiss to tide them over.

"WHAT DO YOU MEAN leave? Now?" Tess asked Anthony when he handed her the clipboard. "But we just got to Santa Fe."

"Let's check in with Ralph and then get out of here."

All her weariness from a long day on the road slipped away. Her muscles had been screaming with restlessness, but she suddenly forgot the spasms and twinges, forgot *everything* but the look on his handsome face.

His bedroom eyes swept over her, an intimate glance that reminded her of the way his mouth had felt on hers when they'd kissed, of the way she'd sighed and impatiently pressed against him. She'd wanted to feel her breasts against his chest.

"Where are we going?"

He tapped the clipboard, motioning for her to sign in, and said, "That's a surprise."

Tess backed away from the check-in table, out of earshot of Ralph, who was munching his way through a plate piled high with burritos and chicos while eavesdropping on every word they said. "Does this have something to do with spending half the day poring over the rally rule book?"

"I was looking for something."

"What?"

He shook his head, a slow smile drawing her gaze to his mouth and filling her head with the memory of what those lips felt like on hers. "If I tell you, I'll give away my surprise. How about you end the interrogation and trust me?"

She'd known he was up to something when he'd read the rule book cover to cover while she'd driven from Dallas to Wichita Falls. Well, she'd said she wanted to make the most of their time together... And there was something about him, something so confidently *male*, that assured her she was going to like his surprises. A little zip of anticipation shot through her, and she signed her name in an illegible scrawl.

"You rank first today, Tess. That should make you happy," Ralph informed her around a mouthful of burrito. "We've got no room problems and some serious New Mexican dishes, so eat up. The locals who catered the buffet cooked enough for an army."

"Thanks," she said absently.

She'd guessed they'd come in with decent standings as the food trays were full, the banquet room empty and it was still early yet. But she didn't get a chance to say anything else when Anthony slipped his hand around her waist and whisked her toward the buffet.

"Make a plate for the road." He grabbed two foam travel boxes provided for the eat-and-runners. She scanned the table of steaming goodies. Plates stacked with tortillas made from multicolored corn. Tureens filled with *calabacitos* and *frijoles refritos* and red chile sauce. Not to mention every garnish from cheese and olives to fresh veggies.

She ladled some colorful bean soup into a cup then

popped a few extra *chile rellenos* into Anthony's box. "Mind if I put these in yours? I don't want to take a box for just a couple."

He cast a sidelong glance at her cup then did a double take. "That's all you're taking? You haven't eaten since lunch."

"I haven't moved since breakfast. This is fine."

He frowned.

"What?"

"We won't have a chance to grab anything later."

She could have argued that a quick trip in the elevator and a few quarters would have made a meal in the hotel's vending machine in the middle of the night, but as she still didn't know what he had planned… "Is this an Italian thing, Anthony?"

"What?"

"Your obsession with what I eat?"

"Obsession? That's harsh…" His voice trailed off as his gaze riveted straight to the mouth in question. "All right. I admit I do think about what you put in your mouth."

Tess just rolled her eyes. "I thought we agreed I didn't need any more mother hens in my life."

"Food is different, *chère*," he drawled. "It's important for you to keep up your strength."

"I haven't seen any reason why yet."

"You will," he whispered close to her ear. "Trust me."

That warm burst of lazy sound shimmered through her and started up the whole craziness inside again, the liquid heat that hadn't quite disappeared since their kiss hours earlier.

His open mouth brushed her ear, and to support his belief, she shivered, one of those full-bodied numbers that there was no way he could have missed.

He gave a throaty chuckle.

She waved goodbye to Ralph as they left the pit stop. "So where to now?"

"The car."

Tess came to a stop in the hallway and closed her eyes. "Oh, please tell me your surprise doesn't involve driving."

"'Fraid so. Can't be helped."

"I can't, Anthony. I just can't. I appreciate what you're doing here, but I'm going to crawl out of my skin if I have to sit in that car again tonight."

She opened her eyes to find him staring down at her, brow arched dispassionately, holding his food box one-handed like a seasoned waiter. "You said you'd trust me."

"But that was before I knew you wanted to get back in the car. I've got to swim or hit the treadmill, some-thing…*anything* to move my muscles before they atro-phy—"

"If you don't like road trips, why do you rally?"

That stopped her in midwhine, and she scowled at him. "I do like road trips. I just need to move."

"Then trust me. The sooner you get in the car, the sooner you'll get out."

"Oh, all right." She gave a huff then took off toward the front lobby and the exit without waiting for him.

When they reached the car, Anthony motioned her to the passenger's side.

"Why don't you let me drive, so you can eat?" she asked.

He popped the box lid to reveal a stack of neatly rolled burritos. "I made mine to go."

She laughed. "I'm impressed. You've really got take-out meals under control."

He slipped behind the wheel then drove out of the parking lot. Tess opened his box and spread a napkin over his lap while he merged with the highway traffic and headed north.

"Thanks." Grabbing a burrito, he skillfully brought it to his mouth without taking his eyes from the road.

"Totally under control," she repeated then sipped her dinner.

They drove in companionable silence for a while, and Tess finally put the lid on the remainder of her soup and fitted it into the cup holder on the utility tray. Anthony made quick work of his burritos, and she finally packed them up, too, watching curiously as he exited off the highway and headed down a one-lane road that looked as if it led to no place she wanted to go.

"Not even a hint?" she asked. "You're driving us into the sticks as if you've been here before."

"I have been here before, but only once. I still need some light to see the road signs."

"Which would explain why you were driving like a maniac today—to outrace the sunset?"

"It would."

She wasn't going to argue, or stress, either. They'd ranked first, after all. And Tess had grown up around cars—between her daddy's background in sales and Uncle Ray—she felt comfortable with the way Anthony handled himself on the road.

The sun set above the firs and juniper pines. Tess thought Texas had the biggest and best piece of sky anywhere she'd ever been, but way up high on New Mexico's plateau, she found this slice of sunset a breathtaking splash of colors.

"So when were you here before?"

"A few years back I took up road trips as a hobby," he said thoughtfully. "Decided I needed to get out of town more often. Long weekends and that sort of thing."

"Cool. So with whom do you take these long weekend trips?" The question was out of her mouth before Tess could consider how he might interpret it. She guessed it didn't really matter, though. She was interested in his love life, and couldn't see any sense pretending she wasn't.

He shifted his gaze off the road and eyed her searchingly. "I took this one with my brother."

"Oh. What's your brother's name?"

"Vinny." Anthony laughed. "He'd kill me if he knew I told a pretty girl his name was Vinny. Nowadays he goes by *Vince*. He has an image to maintain since he's doing his residency."

"Probably doesn't want to sound too young."

Anthony was obviously very fond of this brother, and she didn't think that should surprise her. The Anthony she'd seen during this past week might have been all swagger and cool business, but when she remembered how quickly he'd pointed Uncle Ray in his family's direction for credibility, she guessed they must be close.

"Well, I know you have an older brother in the police department, a younger brother who's a doctor, and a mother who reared you to behave like a gentleman around ladies. Anyone else in the family?"

"Two older brothers, two younger brothers and a baby sister."

"Whoa! *Six* DiLeos." She added a little mock horror for emphasis. "Your poor widowed mother. She had her hands full."

"Oh, yeah, but you'd have never known it. She kept us all in line. She might only be five feet tall, but she's tough."

"Is that an Italian thing, too?"

"Oh, yeah. No one messes with Mama. Marc tried once. " He gave another laugh. "And while she was cooking. The idiot."

"What happened?"

"She hurled a knife. Missed his ear by two inches."

"Bet that was the last time he messed with her."

He nodded. "You should hear him tell the story. Mama just says it was one of her defining moments as a parent. She needed to set an example for her boys. Without my father around, she knew if one challenged her authority, we all would. She's actually pretty funny about it. Especially when she launches into the part about how it doesn't matter how big we grow—she brought us into the world, she can take us back out."

An image of a tiny virago with blond hair and dark eyes and a knife sprang to mind, and she couldn't help but smile. "Sounds like a smart mother. And loving. Courtney sounded very okay with being adopted by your family."

"What's not to be okay with? You should taste my mama's cooking." He kissed his fingers with a juicy *mwah* sound. "She makes a red sauce that'll make you weep."

With a laugh, Tess sank back against the door to get a better look at him in the growing darkness. What was it about this man that felt so good? Here she'd placed him in a situation where most men would have shown their butts the first night, yet he'd entertained her and fretted over her and made her want him even more than she already did.

She was glad when he finally steered off the main road and pulled down the cutaway entrance of a wilderness preserve. A uniformed park ranger stepped out of the gatehouse.

Anthony exhaled heavily. "We made it."

"This is my surprise?" she asked, but didn't get an answer before Anthony rolled down the window to talk with the ranger.

While listening to their exchange, it didn't take long to piece together what was happening—Anthony had reserved spots on the wilderness preserve's popular "night walk," a silent, ranger-led hike through the dark ruins of Indian cliff houses and pueblo-style dwellings.

Tess knew a little about the area—not much, but enough to know the canyon was well over six thousand feet in elevation and the wilderness preserve encompassed a massive amount of northern New Mexico acreage. A hike through this trail would be the perfect way to loosen her muscles and work off restlessness.

And once Anthony pulled through the gate to park in the lighted lot in front of the visitor's center, she told him. He'd barely gotten the car into gear before she'd leaned across the seat and slipped her arms around his neck to kiss his cheek.

"This is a brilliant surprise."

Hiking through the darkness together, enjoying the activity, the clean high-elevation air, the peace and quiet of a starry night after two long days of sitting in the car. She couldn't think of anything better.

"This is only part of my surprise."

"What's the other part?"

"I checked the rule book. There's nothing that says we have to stay at the pit stop hotel."

She tipped her head back to meet his gaze. "I know. The hotel's just a convenience. Room block with a decent rate, and since we have to check in there anyway—"

"We'll spend the night out here in the campground."

The flood lamps outside spilled fractured light through the windshield to make his face a study of shadow and light. Yet still she could see the question in his gaze, knew that her reaction meant something.

"How did you arrange all this?"

"I made some calls when we stopped to pick up lunch."

"But we were together…" Then she remembered. "I thought you were in that bathroom a long time."

He grimaced.

"Are you still trying to impress me?" She scooted closer until she could—almost—press her chest against him.

Lowering his mouth to hers, he brushed his words against her lips like kisses. "I'm really going to impress you tonight."

Tess believed him.

7

Owning a business meant Anthony spent a good deal of time in his service center's office, but he'd never gotten out of the bays completely. He still worked on cars, mostly those of friends and family, not to mention keeping up his Firebird and the Harley-Davidson chopper he'd restored to mint condition over a decade ago. He preferred keeping physically active, so a hike through the ruins proved a perfect warm-up for the night ahead.

He and Tess had walked the trail with twenty other hikers then separated from the group at the visitor's center. Now they followed the ranger's Jeep to the campsite. Tess sat beside him as he drove, looking flushed and beautiful from the activity and curious about the night ahead.

"I haven't seen one campsite in this direction, Anthony. Isn't everything back on the other side of the visitor's center? That's where everyone else was headed."

"Nervous to be alone in the dark with me, *chère?*"

She rolled her eyes. "I've been *waiting* to get you alone in the dark."

Anthony liked how she'd formed her opinion of him then trusted her instincts even though they hadn't known each other long. She'd been on-target about Keene Motors, too, which told him Tess was a very good judge of character.

"There's another campsite on this part of the canyon, but a fire wiped out a portion of the forest a while back and some trails flooded from the rescue efforts. They've been rehabilitating the area."

"And they're letting us camp here? How'd you manage that?"

He chuckled. "It's not as impressive as it sounds, trust me. The rehab is basically over, so they'll be booking campers soon to catch what's left of the season. The other campsite is for conventional campers. Over here is where we yurt. I just talked the Preserve Director into letting us start things up early. We'll only be here for one night, and this is where Vinny and I stayed. I like the view."

"I'll bite. What's yurt?"

"You'll see soon."

She beamed a smile that made his blood start pumping warm and slow with awareness, made him glad he'd thought of this for what would be a first for them—a first night together. A night for seduction. He planned to make love to Tess out in this magnificent place.

When the ranger pulled to a stop and flashed his brights on a wooden sign that read: Piñon Campsite, Anthony pulled along beside him and turned off the ignition.

The ranger stepped out and shined his flashlight in the direction of the trees. "Your site's that way. Just follow the trail, and you can't miss it. It's the only yurt outfitted yet. There's a pit bathroom nearby."

"Great." He ignored the sight of Tess frowning in his periphery. "Tell Jay thanks again for letting me visit on such short notice."

"I'll tell him." The ranger extended his hand and they shook. "But you know Jay. He runs this place like summer camp. Having the yurts down all season has been killing him."

No doubt there. He and Vinny had camped here for a solid week, and during that time had shared some informative, and lively conversations with the preserve director. "Makes for happy return campers."

"Essential for continued funding." He touched the rim of his hat. "You folks have a good night. I left a radio, in case something comes up. This high up, the cell signals get sketchy."

"Thanks." Tess moved close as the ranger got into his Jeep and pulled out in a flash of red taillights. "Pit bathroom?"

"Okay, so it's more rustic than a normal campsite. How about I promise to make it up to you tomorrow night in Vegas?"

"Deal." The word came out on a little hitch of excitement, and Anthony found himself reaching up to touch her face, to trace the full curve of her lower lip.

Tipping her head back, she dragged her mouth against his thumb, a simple but intensely erotic move that made him eager to get to the seduction on the road. "Just bring my carry bag, please. I won't need anything but my toothbrush tonight."

Oh, yeah. He wouldn't even suggest a change of clothes for the trip tomorrow, didn't want the thought of clothes entering the picture now—not when he was picturing her without any.

Grabbing their carry bags, he led Tess into the forest with only the flashlight beam to slice along the dark trail. The wind rustled leaves and scuffles of wildlife broke the silence.

"If we hadn't just done that night walk, I might find this

place a little spooky," she whispered. "It feels like we're the only two people on the planet."

"That was the point, *chère*."

She laughed, a silvery sound that made him smile, and then her eyes grew wide as the flashlight beam cut across the sizable dome that poised majestically overlooking the canyon.

"Oh, Anthony." She breathed his name on a whisper.

"A yurt." Dropping the bags, he touched their flashlight to direct the beam to the ground. "And look at this view. Worth a pit bathroom."

"It's perfect." She exhaled a long sigh—exactly the response he'd wanted. "I had no idea you were so romantic. You're usually all Mr. Macho Driver Man."

"Macho? Please. Romance is an Italian thing." Slipping his arms around her waist, he eased her close for a real kiss, one where he could finally feel her body pressed against him.

She melted into his arms with another soft sigh, fitting against him with almost magical precision. Her breasts molded his chest, her sleek curves pressed against all his right places, her long legs rested perfectly between his.

Grazing his hands along her back, he tested the supple lines of her spine, ran his palms along the curve of her waist. He wanted to discover Tess tonight, explore the way she made him feel, learn how to coax those little sighs from her lips.

To his pleasure, she arched backward and looped her arms around his neck. Her stomach cradled what was swiftly becoming an erection, and he pressed his mouth to hers, tasting the way sensation mingled a slow kiss with a rapid-fire surge of heat straight to his crotch.

Her sigh broke against his mouth. He slid his tongue inside, tangled it with hers. She snuggled against him, bombarding him with soft breasts against his chest, muscles gathering as her stomach rode his erection. She spread her legs just enough to keep her balance, and instinctively, he wedged his thigh between. The loose cotton shorts she wore left very little to the imagination. He could feel a warmth radiating outward, penetrating, promising.

Then she rode his thigh in one sleek stroke.

There was no missing the way she melted in his arms, no missing that she'd found a pleasure point. So he slipped his hand down to cup her bottom and helped her ride that next stroke, his erection surging almost painfully when she deepened their kiss and ground against him.

This woman was fire and he'd never guessed how much he'd thrill to the challenge of meeting her, dare for dare, of earning her interest and winning her trust and claiming her enthusiasm as the ultimate prize.

If he kissed her anymore right now, he'd lose it, and they'd be naked quicker than he could say, "Start your engines." And he wanted so much more for his first time with Tess. He couldn't keep running his hands over her body or get lost in the way she pressed against him in sexy invitation.

He needed to put on the brakes, so in a quick move, he scooped her into his arms.

She laughed against his mouth and hung on. Bending over, he held her tight so she could retrieve the flashlight and they stepped inside. She sliced the beam around to reveal a sparse interior and the most unique feature of a yurt—the acrylic skylight.

"All right, Jay." He scanned the air mattress covering enough of the floor to make a regular love nest, along with serviceable sheets, blankets and pillows.

"Wow," Tess said. "Much better than a night in a hotel. Especially after being cooped up inside a car for two days."

"My thoughts exactly." He rolled her out of his arms and onto the mattress, where she bounced with more silvery laughter. He flopped down beside her. "I was hoping a born and bred Texan would enjoy a night outdoors, since ya'll invented the concept of sleeping under the big sky."

"True, true. But I want to know who came up with this whole yurt thing. It's brilliant."

"If memory serves, Jay told us it was the Mongolians. Animal hides over wooden frames. Rustic and practical."

"Wow." She turned the flashlight off with a flick and cast their world into blackness. "No more light. I need my eyes to adjust. I've got some things I want to see in the dark."

"And what are they?" Anthony's night vision hadn't kicked in yet, but he didn't need sight. His body honed in on hers like a beacon. "The stars? The canyon? The trees?"

She flipped on top of him, and he pulled her into his arms, using touch to find his way, liking how the springy air mattress contoured to their bodies so they might have been wrapped around each other on a cloud.

"I want to see skin." Her body spread out against him, all sleek hollows and valleys of unfamiliar terrain he'd been dying to explore. "*Your* skin, Anthony. All of it."

Tess didn't ask permission but dragged her hands along his stomach until she found the hem of his shirt.

"Lean up," she urged, and Anthony propped himself up on his elbows, moving from side to side as she maneuvered the shirt over his head.

Her fingers glanced his skin and sparked fire in their wake. He tried to pull her back into his arms but she braced her hands on his chest and resisted.

"Not so fast. I'm not done looking yet."

"Your wish…" Hooking his hands behind his head, he stretched out. His night sight had adjusted enough so he could see her face and appreciate the pleasure he saw there.

And when she pushed herself up to straddle him, she made him thank whatever lucky star was shining on him that he'd pursued her. He didn't care whether his Auto-TexCare plan ever saw the light of day, not when Tess spread her legs over his erection and rode him a slow, hard stroke.

"This would be so perfect if we were naked." Her voice was an aching whisper in the darkness.

"That can be arranged."

She spread her thighs a little wider, pressing down on him in a sensual way that made him groan aloud. "All in good time."

She obviously wanted to play things her way, and as his crotch throbbed and his hands itched to grab her, Anthony would let her. He would try, at least. He couldn't promise anything as she dipped her fingers into the scoop between his neck and shoulders and massaged the muscles there, a firm motion that eased away tension and added to the languid way he felt.

Languid didn't last long.

Tess reared back and whipped her shirt over her head, taking her bra along with it. His heartbeat stalled in his chest as her pale breasts bounced free. Her nipples were smudges in the darkness, and the urge to reach out and cup their soft weight in his palms hit him hard. He wanted to drag those pouty nipples into his mouth, hear her moan in pleasure.

But Tess was the only one who moved.

She sank forward, a liquid motion that brought all that

smooth skin against his chest. He could feel the tips tighten as they traveled his skin, caught in his chest hairs, slow, tantalizing movements that nearly laid him low.

He groaned, unable to stop himself, fighting the urge to grab her, to press his crotch into her heat. She leaned a little closer, let her breasts swell against him, a soft fullness that brought skin against skin and made him clench his fingers together to resist touching her.

He buried his face in her hair instead, sucked in deep breaths of that sultry vanilla-almond mingled with the underlying scent of this woman who aroused him so completely.

She lifted up enough to skim her hands beneath her, threading her fingers through the hairs on his chest, tugging lightly as she went, evoking fire.

"I knew all this sexy gold hair would turn me on," she whispered.

He hadn't realized his mesh shirts, which were comfortable in the summer heat, were so see-through.

Or had Tess just been looking *that* closely?

Anthony didn't get a chance to enjoy the thought long because she chose that moment to slither her tongue inside his ear, and muscles all over his body contracted in response.

She gave a whispery laugh.

Against his ear, of course, which made all those muscles contract again.

"Oh, I like this, Anthony. We're fire together."

"Did you doubt it?" He sounded casual, in control, when he felt far from it.

"Not for a second. It's been forever since I've had any life signs. I thought something was wrong—until I met you."

That made him laugh, stoked some inner part of him that liked hearing how he'd done what no other man had lately. Especially Keene Motors.

Slipping his hands around her, he treated himself to the feel of her skin, skidding his fingers over her shoulders, along her arms, down her back. He teased himself by thumbing the sides of her breast, savored her reaction when she shivered. Not from cold because it was getting damn hot in this yurt.

She traced the shell of his ear with her tongue, exhaled a sigh, taunted him with her wispy breaths.

This was another game they played. Give and take. Control and submit. Thrill or be thrilled. And each part had its appeal. Touching Tess or letting Tess touch him.

Anthony liked it both ways.

So he dragged his hands down her rib cage into the scoop of her waist, over the swell of her hips, feeling, learning, savoring her smooth skin beneath his hands, the way she breathed against his ear.

He rounded the curve of her bottom, his fingers digging into cheeks enough to press her closer… Anthony couldn't resist. He ground his erection into the soft swell of her heat.

She let out a half moan, half sigh—or maybe he'd made the sound? He didn't know. He only knew that fire surged through him, and he could do nothing but anchor her close and grind against her once more, a hard thrust that mimicked the real thing.

His intensity seemed to spark Tess from her daze, and she dragged her open mouth down his neck, nipping his jaw along the way, making him vibrate with each playful bite.

He rode her again, stunned at the strength of his need. He'd always appreciated a good orgasm, but this brushfire heat was almost too hot to handle. When she slithered away from him, he groaned.

She raised her arms to sweep her hair back from her shoulders, giving him a shot of her naked upper body in all its glory. Her breasts thrust proudly. Her smile seemed both bold and thoughtful as she raked her gaze over him.

"One of us needs to lose more clothes," she said. "I think it's getting kind of warm in here."

He'd had that exact thought. To his profound pleasure, he watched her go for the button at her waist and shimmy out of her shorts in a series of moves that made her breasts sway. She dragged her panties along for the ride, and when the jumble of clothing caught at her knees, he asked, "Need my help?"

"Hmph." She rolled backward on the air mattress and drew her knees up, giving him a shot of her pale cheeks and making him wish for more light so he could enjoy everything the darkness hid.

He sat up, unable to resist touching her bottom, tracing the smooth curve of skin with his open hand, the line of firm muscle down her thigh. She kicked her clothes over the side then scooted out of reach.

"Hey," he protested. "I was enjoying myself."

"Me, too." Rolling off the mattress, she rose to her feet in a fluid move.

Anthony could only stare in dazed appreciation, momentarily blinded by the sight of this woman in all her naked glory.

She was exquisite. With the tumble of dark hair flowing over her shoulders and down her back and long shapely legs, she was gorgeous in an earthy, natural way he found so appealing.

"You're so beautiful, Tess."

It was trite. It was probably something she'd heard from every man she'd ever brought to his knees. But Anthony meant it. It was a simple truth that held a lot of power.

"Thank you."

No sassy comeback. No coyness, either, as far as he could tell. She had him by the balls and knew it, but respected him for being there. He liked her confidence. It radiated off her as she stood before him so at ease with her body in a way so many women would never be.

He liked that she eyed him so hungrily.

"Anthony, will you drag the mattress outside? I want to lay in your arms with the cool breeze running across my skin."

He extended his hand to her. "Help me up."

As soon as she slipped her fingers into his, Anthony levered his weight against hers and pulled her down beside him.

She landed against him in a tumble of laughter. Silky skin glanced against him, a thigh, a hip, a soft breast, and each galvanized the ache inside him. But he forced himself to stand.

He laughed to find his knees like rubber, but he didn't give her a chance to notice before skirting the mattress and kneeling down to give a push. "Hang on."

She rolled onto her stomach, spread her arms wide and grabbed the edges to brace herself.

"I'm going to dream about the sight of you like this every time I close my eyes for the rest of my life," he said.

"Glad you like the view." Then she spread her legs wide, hooking her toes on the mattress sides, teasing him with glimpses of places he couldn't fully see in the darkness.

He had everything he could do not to sink down on top of her, cover every inch of her sexy body with his. With another hearty push, he sent her jolting through the yurt flap.

He had to squeeze past the mattress to finish the job, but realized the benefits of being outside instantly. "You glow in silver out here, *chère*. You don't even look real."

She propped herself up on an elbow and looked surreal, spread out before him in the starlight, the wind whipping tendrils of hair around her face and neck.

"Cold?"

She raised her arms to him. "Come warm me."

He was beside her in an instant, savoring the way her body unfolded against him, all his fantasies realized when her legs twined through his and she threaded her arms around him, crushing her breasts to his chest.

He skimmed his hands down the length of her arms, around her back, felt the goose bumps on her skin. He brought his leg around her and anchored her close.

"Kiss me, Anthony."

"You say that a lot."

"I like the way you kiss."

"Lucky for me." Slipping his fingers around her jaw, he eased her face upward, a deliberate move that let him study her features in the starlight.

Thick lashes fringing eyes that seemed almost black in the shadows, the creamy skin, the pouty mouth so ready for his kisses. Then she let her eyes flutter shut and her lips parted on a sigh, a murmur carried off by a burst of wind.

He lowered his face to hers, savoring the anticipation as he closed in. Then his mouth touched hers, without the confinement of a cramped car to hinder movement, with the freedom to explore and the promise of the whole night ahead.

This kiss was the real deal.

This kiss allowed for roving hands and twined legs and thrusting hips. This kiss wound their tension tighter as the night wheeled around them, a heady combination of canyon wind and starlit shadow and loamy forest.

Of promise.

Of passion.

Anthony could smell desire, Tess's, his own. He could feel their hunger escalating in the way their hands traveled over each other in a frenzy.

And when she broke their kiss to trail her mouth along his jaw, down his throat, sucking gently on his pulse point, Anthony knew a need that went beyond the thrill of the moment, went beyond physical excitement... This kiss made him *want*.

He reached for the button that fastened his jeans, but Tess stopped him.

"No, let me. I've been wanting to see what you keep hidden in here since you nudged me out of first place on the track."

Her voice edged with excitement, her words bold and honest.

"Should I be worried?"

"Vengeance isn't my speed." She laughed. "This'll be a search-and-rescue operation."

He sucked in a hard breath as her fingers grazed his stomach. "Ah, man, Tess. Rescue away."

She unzipped his fly and slipped her fingers inside his briefs to maneuver the whole deal free. Her intimate touch made it impossible to hold back, and when she moved down his body, a vision better than any fantasy with all her pale skin gleaming, he couldn't keep his hands off her.

He stroked her breasts, her shoulders, her face, *everything* he could reach. But she wouldn't be sidetracked. She worked the tangle of clothes from his hips while he hiked his butt off the mattress to help her rescue his lower half.

He finally kicked his pants free. "It's damn cold out here without clothes, *chère*. I've got body parts shriveling up."

"Nothing we can't unshrivel with a little effort."

Very little effort, no doubt. But he didn't tell Tess. Let her work to please him. He couldn't think of a thing better.

"My wallet. Grab it from my pocket."

"Protection?"

He nodded.

She'd no sooner grabbed his wallet and tossed his jeans back into the yurt than he grabbed her.

"Anthony." She bounced down onto the mattress and tried to roll away.

She didn't stand a chance.

"I've wanted to feel you naked since the day we met."

"Really?"

"You're haunting my dreams, *chère*."

Apparently those were the magic words because she stopped resisting. But Tess had her own plan. Swinging her leg around, she straddled him again, sitting on his thighs, her woman's softness teasing him with her heat.

"I want to play Queen of the Mountain."

"How about Queen of the High Elevation? This is a canyon. Technically, there's a difference."

She laughed, the real woman far more gorgeous than

any dream. She had the sleek body of an active woman, all toned muscles and creamy skin that flashed and shone when she held up his wallet. "Do you mind? I want to do the honors."

"Be still my heart."

She met his gaze, eyes sparkling as she rummaged through his wallet to produce a foil square.

"Got it." She sent the wallet sailing behind her, through the open flap, where it clattered against…a lantern?

"Bull's eye," he said around a tight breath as she tore open the packet and honed in on his crotch.

But she wasn't ready to get straight to business. Slipping her fingers beneath his balls, she cupped him with a firm touch, weighing the guys in her warm palm to reawaken his body.

"Ah, Tess."

"Like that, do you?"

A rhetorical question because she couldn't possibly expect him to reply while she was dragging her fingers up his length. All he could do was hold himself brutally still. His dick swelled, and when she hooked her fingers beneath the head and gave a playful tug, his whole body jerked in reply.

"That's a hot spot." She did it again.

"You do realize if you keep doing that, I'm going to have to get you back, don't you?" He sounded a lot more controlled than he felt.

Another sharp tug.

Another full-bodied spasm that made her laugh.

"Vengeance, hmm? You're welcome to try, of course."

Anthony locked his hands around her waist and was about to show her a view of the sky from on her back, but she slid her fingers around his dick and hung on.

Pressing his head into the mattress, he let go fast enough.

"Now lie still." She worked the condom onto him in less than precise moves, and he smiled. He liked that for all her boldness he still had the ability to fluster her.

"A night outdoors was sheer brilliance," she said. "Now stop distracting me and let me thank you properly."

With a neat move she positioned herself and levered him against her heat. He skimmed along her body in a path of moisture, penetrating just enough to make him ache.

Her sigh and his groan collided in the night air.

She rose naked above him, her hair whipping out on the wind, her body gleaming silver. He reached up to cup her breasts in his hands, pinching her nipples, winning a response when she took aim and sank down.

She was hot and tight and stretched around him as though their bodies had been designed to fit together. She gave a full-bodied shiver and arched forward, the motion driving him inside even deeper. And the sight of her poised above him, her pale thighs straining as she rode up for another stroke…

The tumble of shiny hair in the darkness, strands whipping around her face and playing around her shoulders…

The warm breasts swelling against his palms…

The tightness of her wet heat clenching him in deliberate spasms that were making it impossible not to thrust upward, short driving strokes that made her gasp whimpery sounds, made his tension wind so tight he couldn't stop.

He tugged her nipples, as much to distract her as him, but evasive maneuvers were useless. Their bodies came together with no reference to how long he might want to make this moment last.

She rode him hard, again and again, and he locked his hands around her waist to lend speed to her efforts, unable to shut his eyes at the sight she made rocking sensually above him, breasts bouncing, bottom swaying to a rhythm he could feel through every nerve in his body.

He was on fire, his whole body consumed by her, and when she cried out, a sound of pure pleasure that disappeared on the wind, he went a little crazy, driving inside, wild with the way her sex spasmed around him, the way she gasped on each upstroke as if he forced the sound out with each thrust.

She didn't shy from him, but embraced the intensity of the moment, digging her fingers into his chest to steel herself and ride him as he growled out his pleasure, exploding.

Anthony didn't know when he'd closed his eyes. He had no idea when she'd collapsed on top of him. He only knew that she draped over him in a tangle of glorious woman, and he felt more contented, more *alive,* than he'd felt in so long.

He ran his hands along her to memorize the feel of each sleek curve, to capture everything about the way he felt.

She finally said, "Anthony, I'm freezing."

He laughed, a heartfelt sound that echoed down into the canyon and far off into the night.

8

TESS WAS STILL RIDING the weary glow from the night past, sipping her Starbucks coffee and contentedly watching the sky pale in streaks of a pastel sunrise. She would have loved to see the dawn over the canyon and decided she'd go back again to do just that—perhaps on the drive home, when they weren't crushed for time.

A smile tugged at her lips. She liked the sound of a sunrise in Anthony's arms. They deserved another special night together to make up for the one they'd lost.

She watched him as he drove, clipping along with the predawn traffic on the two-lane road they'd taken out of Santa Fe. For two days, they'd chatted constantly, getting to know each other, but this morning, they just drove along in companionable silence as the terrain rushed past in a blur of fading shadows.

Tess liked the quiet. It was filled with the warm familiarity of the night past, a lingering closeness that was somehow unexpected. She might not have dated in a while, but she'd had relationships before. Mornings after could be filled with a rush of new passion or tenderly awkward, almost too new. None had ever felt like this, breathless and...*inevitable*.

That surprised her the most. How satisfied she felt right

now, how comfortable she was sitting beside this man after all the intimacies they'd shared last night.

How eager she was to spend more time together.

He finally noticed her watching him. "What?"

"I was just thinking about last night."

A smile touched his mouth, too, and she liked the drowsy warmth that crept through her at the sight, liked having the power to please him.

Tess was still mulling her reaction to these unexpectedly warm and fuzzy feelings when the electronic jangle of her cell phone chimed over the hum of the car's engine.

She grabbed it from the utility tray, and glanced at the display. "Hi, Daddy."

"Good morning, sugar." His forceful voice seemed almost too big for the satellite signal. "Sleep well last night?"

"Never better."

"Pleased to hear it. Mind telling me *where* you slept that I couldn't reach you by cell."

Uh-oh. "At about six thousand feet. The ranger said the cell coverage might be sketchy."

That earned her a dubious glance from Anthony.

"You were camping?" Daddy asked, sounding as dubious as Anthony looked.

"We went for a night tour of the canyon. After two days in this car, we needed to get out and move around—it was gorgeous. That's why I forgot to check in. Sorry I worried you."

Anthony was frowning now, and Tess reached over to pat his knee. This was her fault, not his. She should have called to let her daddy know they'd decided to bypass the pit stop hotel.

"Another letter was waiting for me when I came in from

the office yesterday. I wanted you and that young man of yours to be on red alert."

"Oh no, Daddy. What did it say?"

"It asked me how I felt about my nearest and dearest heading out of town and leaving me alone."

That gave even her a chill. Whoever was sending these letters was watching their family a little too closely for comfort. She could just imagine her daddy finding this letter when he'd walked in the door from the office. He always came in late from his managers meeting on Monday nights, so he'd have tried to call her. No dice on her cell. Most likely he'd tried Anthony's cell, too. No dice there, either. He would have tried the scheduled pit stop hotel only to be told that she hadn't checked in….

"Didn't sleep last night, did you?" She already guessed the answer.

"'Fraid not. There's just something about knowing this crazy is watching my family close enough to know they are scattered like fleas on a dog's bath day that had me a bit unsettled."

A *bit* was putting it mildly. "Is Glen having any luck tracking down this one?" she asked, referring to Daddy's chief of security at AutoCarTex.

"He's working on it. This one came postmarked from Little Rock. Haven't had one from there before. So that's new."

Anthony must have gotten the gist of the conversation because suddenly he was motioning her to cover the mouthpiece so he could talk.

"Hang on a sec, Daddy," she said. "What?"

"Tell him that we won't be staying at the pit stop hotel tonight, either. Tell him we'll go five-star, and I'll explain the situation to security so they're on the lookout. We'll call and tell him where as soon as I book the reservation."

Tess relayed the message, knowing this was exactly what Daddy needed to hear right now. Anthony had just earned a few points with her. Probably with her daddy, too. And to her surprise, she really didn't mind.

Alerting security to a potential problem was a good idea, even if it did remind her that Anthony was all about winning her daddy's respect and approval for his Auto-TexCare plan. She hadn't wanted any reminders during their break from reality, but somehow it didn't rankle so much when she heard her daddy's sigh of relief on the other end of the connection.

"Let me know your plans as soon as you make them, sugar. I'll be waiting."

"I will."

"Have a good drive, and stay safe."

"Love you, Daddy."

"Love you, too, sugar." She blew kisses into the receiver then disconnected to find Anthony watching her as she set the phone back in the utility tray.

"Tell me all about these letters, Tess."

"Don't want anything to happen on your watch, hmm?"

His gaze narrowed, and that mouth she'd kissed so intimately last night straightened into a grim line. "I don't want anything happening to you at all."

"I AM SO READY for that shower," Anthony whispered to Tess when the hotel desk clerk moved toward the computer to pull up their reservation for their night in Las Vegas.

"You don't have to tell me," Tess said. "I've been stuck in a car with you all day, remember?"

Anthony blinked, and she had to struggle to keep hold of her deadpan expression. Fortunately, the uniformed desk clerk provided a distraction.

"There's been a change to your reservation."

"What change? I talked to your general manager and security chief making these arrangements."

Anthony got attentive fast. Probably worried about his shower. She hadn't been kidding. The man needed one. After a night spent making love under the stars and a day baking in the car, he smelled like a heady combination of ripe male and sex.

It had been all she could do to keep her hands off him during the long drowsy hours on the road. In fact, she hadn't been able to, Tess remembered with a mental sigh. Being together had driven away all thoughts of worrisome letters and concerned family members.

Even after Anthony had made the arrangements for tonight's stay, they'd tried to take turns napping to make up for an exhausting night, but sleep hadn't come to either of them. They'd both been suffering a serious case of *lust*sickness, and she remembered one particularly memorable stretch of desert road when she'd tested Anthony's driving skill by entertaining herself in his lap.

She hadn't been able to help herself, and decided his strong male smell wouldn't let her stop thinking about sex. Every time she'd stretch out on the bench seat, she'd find herself staring up at him, his chiseled jaw, the strong hands he rested easily on the steering wheel, and remembering how he'd felt inside her every time they'd made love last night.

"Let me double-check when this change was made and by whom." The clerk tapped out a rapid-fire burst of keystrokes.

Anthony glanced down at her, a brow arched in tenuous patience. A little thrill coursed through her as his golden-brown eyes trailed over her face, a gesture that assured her he was just as eager to get into their hotel room as she was.

He discreetly slipped his hand into hers, a gesture she found sweet. Then he bent low, so his mouth practically brushed her ear. "I'm looking forward to giving you a shower."

Her sex gave a needy little twinge in reply, and she smiled. "Me, too."

She hoped the trouble would be easily resolved. Anthony had been insistent about not staying in the pit stop hotel tonight, so he'd made this reservation from his cell phone en route. Everything had seemed pretty straightforward.

The clerk finally said, "I see what happened. The general manager upgraded your room to one of our presidential suites."

Anthony frowned. "You're sure?"

"Reservation for two under DiLeo?" There was a question in his voice as he shifted his gaze between them.

"That part's right," Tess said. "But why would your manager upgrade our room?"

The clerk opened his mouth to reply, but then a beautiful redheaded woman approached and said, "Security reasons, and he's sucking up to you."

She and Anthony exchanged glances, not sure what to make of the woman. She didn't seem alarming with her bright smile and professional blue silk suit.

"I understand the security reasons, but why would he suck up to us?" Anthony asked.

"Because his wife is a reporter with the *Vegas Times-Press*. She's been keeping track of all the rally contestants to see if any bypassed the pit stop hotel. When she heard contestants booked a reservation for tonight and needed additional security, she wanted an interview for an article. So he's doing his bit to make his wife happy."

"By putting us in a presidential suite?" Anthony asked.

"Gratis. They're the best suites in the house, and their floor has its own security monitoring station."

"I assume you're the wife," Tess said.

"Tori Grant." She extended her hand and launched into a cheery explanation. "My husband's sales director contacted the Rally Committee about hosting your pit stop. I have a daily column and want to feature the rally with something more than the typical spin the car club's giving the press. I thought it would be a good way to get the benefiting charity a little more promotion with readers who wouldn't otherwise be interested."

Good promotion for the AutoCarTex Foundation, too. Although Tess didn't think she needed to point that out to Tori Grant. This reporter didn't seem to miss a trick.

"While I'm not on the Rally Committee, I am a car club board member," Tess said. "I know there was concern at our general meeting about the casino. As rally hosts, the Nostalgic Car Club assumes a certain amount of liability. Our contestants sign on to drive a long haul in a short time, and we want them to be fresh when they're on the road, and safe, of course. We generally avoid hotels with nighttime entertainment. Avoiding temptation so to speak."

She hadn't avoided nighttime entertainment or temptation, though. She'd invited hers to make the drive with her.

"That's what I told Adam," Tori said. "But when I heard

you'd booked a room, I thought I'd give an interview another shot. So what do you say? Will you answer a few questions? The article won't run until long after you've left town if you're worried about security."

"We won't be around long enough to give an interview," Anthony said.

"We need to be on the road at the crack of dawn."

"My interview won't take long. I'll bring you up to your room, and we'll be done by the time you've gotten the grand tour and the bellman delivers your bags." She motioned to the desk clerk who immediately handed her their room key. "Sound good?"

Tess glanced up at Anthony, who shrugged, then said, "All right."

Tori Grant was as good as her word. She skillfully masqueraded her interview behind a casual conversation about the rally while escorting them through the hotel.

While standard Las Vegas casino fare, the Parisian leaned more toward upscale than flash. The French romance theme evidenced itself in everything from the five-star service to the stylized period decor.

Cherrywood, gilded decoration and rich colors hallmarked the Parisian's luxury interior, and Tess felt as though they'd stepped through a time warp into some elaborate European palace. She tried not to be distracted by her surroundings as they talked, but found herself glad Anthony, as a first-time contestant, provided a foil to her AutoCarTex Foundation public relations interpretation of the event.

Tori Grant seemed to appreciate the angle, too, because she skillfully zeroed in on their differing impressions of the rally, the contestants and the benefiting charity.

A little part of Tess couldn't help but be surprised by Anthony. Though the man wore a two-day stubble and smelled far from fresh, he segued into Mr. Charming Professional as fast as if he'd flipped a switch.

She'd met him in a casual convention setting and had only glimpsed his business persona when he'd presented his AutoTexCare plan. Otherwise, he'd been laid-back and very adaptable, and it surprised her to watch him slip into that professional role as easily as…well, as easily as *she* did.

Of course a lot of her surprise had to do with seeing his smile. Even though he sounded so contemplative and intelligent, whenever she looked at that dashing grin, she couldn't help but remember all the amazing things he could do with his mouth.

And those memories not only made her heart beat faster, but forced Tess to wonder why she had it so bad for this man.

The answer to that question was a no-brainer. One night alone together had *not* been enough. Not even close. She needed to get Anthony alone again to work off more of this excess lust that had been building since the moment she'd set eyes on him.

One glimpse inside the presidential suite, and Tess knew they'd come to the right place.

After their night in a yurt on a canyon top, this luxury suite seemed as different as a mustang from a mule. The foyer and sitting room continued the period glamour marking the rest of the hotel, but this suite had been furnished with costly antiques and fashionable porcelain pieces that lent to the impression of luxury.

The living room boasted French doors opening onto a

courtyard balcony that overlooked the sparkling terrain of Las Vegas at night. Curtains were fringed, swagged and decorated with tassels. Upholstered chairs and sofas were trimmed in similar fashion as the curtains. Bold-colored carpets covered polished wooden floors.

"Wow," was all Tess could say.

"French styles revived in the nineteenth century were identified by the kings' names who ruled when they were first used," Tori told them. "This is Louis XV. You can tell because he liked S- and C-shaped scrolls like these."

Tess gingerly touched one such scroll on a light that was part of a set flanking a gilded mirror. "I'm impressed. Is interior design a hobby of yours, Tori, or history?"

"Neither actually, but being married to the general manager of this hotel…"

"Got it." And Tess did. Whenever her father and Uncle Ray started talking cars or racing or AutoCarTex… She glanced around at Anthony, who was no slouch in this department, either. She'd learned enough about Anthony DiLeo Automotive in the past few days to get a job there.

They chatted with Tori about their plans for tomorrow's run, and when a knock sounded on the door, Anthony answered it to find the bellman with their bags.

"Okay, that's my cue." Tori extended her hand to Tess and thanked them both. "I'll leave a copy of my article for you when you check out in the morning. You'll have a chance to let me know what you think before it goes to print."

Then she left with the bellman, and they were alone.

Tess wasn't sure what she'd been expecting after she and Anthony finally made it to their hotel. And now that she thought about it, she realized that her sex-soaked brain hadn't been capable of thinking past her immediate need to get clean.

They needed to eat, too. And sleep definitely.

What she didn't expect was for Anthony to sneak up behind her and hoist her off her feet. Suddenly, she came smack up against strong arms, hard chest and sweaty neck.

"Argh, you big, stinky man. What are you doing?"

"Giving you a shower. You stink, too."

"Hmph." The sound only made him laugh as he maneuvered her through the doorway to the master bedroom.

The bedroom proved no less elaborate than the rest of the suite with more French doors and a tall antique bed with a cherrywood step.

"Now let's see what we have." He made another turn to head into the bathroom. "I'm gunning for a garden tub with jets."

"Be forewarned, stinky man. I will *not* get in any standing water with you until you've showered. A few hours ago you were sexy. Now you're on the bad side of ripe."

Without warning, he dragged his tongue up her cheek, a big slurpy lick that made her cringe. "You still taste sexy, *chère.*" Before she could reply, he stopped short in the doorway, forcing her to hang on tight. "Oh, yeah."

Oh, yeah was right.

The bathroom had all kinds of gold froufrou fixtures that gleamed against the white porcelain tile. And the double sink and separate lavatory were convenient, too. But the highlight of this room was the shower stall behind a glass wall large enough to host a party. Tiled with wall jets, a bench ran along two walls, turning the stall into a private sauna.

"No garden tub," she said.

An Important Message from the Editors

Dear Reader,

If you'd enjoy reading romance novels with larger print that's easier on your eyes, let us send you *TWO FREE HARLEQUIN INTRIGUE® NOVELS* in our *NEW LARGER-PRINT EDITION*. These books are complete and unabridged, but the type is set about 25% bigger to make it easier to read. Look inside for an actual-size sample.

By the way, you'll also get a surprise gift with your two free books!

Pam Powers

Peel off Seal and Place Inside...

LARGER-PRINT
FREE BOOKS
EDITION

THE RIGHT WOMAN

she'd thought she was fine. It took Daniel's words and Brooke's question to make her realize she was far from a full recovery.

She'd made a start with her sister's help and she intended to go forward now. Sarah felt as if she'd been living in a darkened room and some- one had suddenly opened a door, letting in the fresh air and sunshine. She could feel its warmth slowly seeping into the coldest part of her. The feeling was liberating. She realized it was only a small step and she had a long way to go, but she was ready to face life again with Serena and her family behind her.

All too soon, they were saying goodbye and arah experienced a moment of sadness for all e years she and Serena had missed. But they d each other now and that's what She held

PRINTED IN THE U.S.A.
Publisher acknowledges the copyright holder of the excerpt from this individual work as follows:
THE RIGHT WOMAN Copyright © 2004 by Linda Warren. All rights reserved.
® and TM are trademarks owned and used by the trademark owner and/or its licensee.

The Harlequin Reader Service™ — Here's How It Works:

Accepting your 2 free Harlequin Intrigue® larger-print books and gift places you under no obligation to buy anything. You may keep the books and gift and return the shipping statement marked "cancel." If you do not cancel, about a month later we'll send you 6 additional Harlequin Intrigue larger-print books and bill you just $4.49 each in the U.S., or $5.24 each in Canada, plus 25¢ shipping & handling per book and applicable taxes if any.* That's the complete price and — compared to cover prices of $5.24 each in the U.S. and $6.24 each in Canada — it's quite a bargain! You may cancel at any time, but if you choose to continue, every month we'll send you 6 more books, which you may either purchase at the discount price or return to us and cancel your subscription.

*Terms and prices subject to change without notice. Sales tax applicable in N.Y. Canadian residents will be charged applicable provincial taxes and GST.

"I'll live."

Given the expression on his handsome face, she guessed Anthony would do a lot more than live. He lowered her to her feet with a sigh and strode to the stall, whipped open the door and popped his head inside. "Twelve jets, Tess. This was definitely worth a fifteen-minute interview. We lucked out."

Tess was thinking along a similar vein as she admired his tight butt when he leaned forward to turn on the jets. A crazy zip of pleasure hummed through her, an almost giddy reaction to a man she'd enjoyed so completely last night.

"Do I need to grab our things?" she asked.

"Don't bother. Everything's in here."

Ah, the luxury of being pampered.

She wouldn't have traded one second of last night, but after their playful stripteases in the great outdoors, tonight's hasty disrobing seemed a joke by comparison. But they were eager. All right, *desperate.* Thirty-six hours was way too long to go without a shower as far as Tess was concerned, but as much as she'd enjoyed peeling off this man's clothes last night, she couldn't deny that watching Anthony tear off his clothes without preamble was downright sexy, too.

Especially when he disappeared beneath the near violent spray, all those muscles flashing, all that golden skin gleaming against the backdrop of tile.

The man literally stole her breath. Yes, he was gorgeous, but it was more than just gorgeous. It was the way looking at him affected her with those shivery feelings inside, a feeling that made her hold her breath to see what would happen next.

Stepping inside the shower, Tess lost herself beneath the

spray, ignoring the man who scrubbed vigorously only a foot away. The hot water pounded over her head and on muscles that felt the effects of too many cramped hours in a car, too many days at a convention running her sleep tank on fumes and a whole glorious night spent in her lover's arms.

The water pounded her into a daze and lather washed away the remnants of sex and sweat. She willed herself to revive so she could enjoy some of their night in this suite before collapsing on the plush bed and passing out. She was so deep into her internal pep talk that she jumped when a hard and thick male body part pressed squarely against her butt.

This body part needed no introduction, even if the rest of the man himself hadn't immediately followed, all strong, *clean* muscles surrounding her as he wrapped his arms around her.

"Mmm. You smell a lot better."

His chest heaved on a deep breath. "You, too."

Tess nestled her bottom against him, gratified when that hard erection surged. "Feeling more awake now, I take it?"

"Oh, yeah." To prove the point, he slithered his hand along her stomach, a glancing caress that made her muscles contract. Spearing his fingers into the hair between her thighs, he earned a shiver. "You, too, hmm?"

"Keep touching me like this, and the answer will be yes."

He chuckled, a throaty sound against her ear.

And he touched her again.

His calloused fingertip slipped between her sensitive folds to zero in on the nub of nerve endings hidden between, an exquisite friction that made her rock back against him and earn another chuckle.

He rolled that little hot spot around, and the pleasure came fast and furious. Tess let her eyes flutter shut and sank back, only vaguely aware of the way he rocked his hips to wedge that thickness between her cheeks and ride his own ache.

Trailing his mouth along her ear, he pressed kisses there, light touches that were as potent as the combined sensations of his skillful fingers and steamy water pounding over them.

She just stood there, allowing it all to wash over her with the water, amazed at the way her body leaped to life with an intensity she could honestly say she'd never felt before. Something about the way she and Anthony came together was so different, so easy. *Right.*

She could only marvel at the way her sex gathered in a slow squeeze as he lazily rolled her hot spot as if the only thing in the world he wanted to do was pleasure her.

And perhaps tonight he did.

He reached for the soap with his free hand then started at her neck, lathering her in lazy circles. Her knees turned to jelly as he massaged that bar around her breasts, more languid motion that made her nipples pucker beneath the spray.

Resting his cheek on the top of her head, he arched his hips to give his erection another slow push. She could feel the heat of his skin, the strength of his arousal, and she trembled at the erotic sensation.

Anthony didn't say a word as he swirled the soap over her ribs and along her stomach. He just cradled her close and touched her as if he wanted to learn her by heart.

And Tess was content to let him. Drowsy and replete, all this warm pleasure swirling inside, the heat building slowly. The reality of this handsome man stoking her passion seemed dreamily unreal right now. When he stopped the languid rolling motion, she tried to rally the energy to protest, but ever the gentleman, Anthony didn't abandon her. He lathered his hands, returned the soap and slipped his fingers between her legs.

"Oh!" she exhaled the sound on a gasp.

His fingers glided through her intimate folds, slick strokes that separated her skin and made her squirm. The memory of his sexy attention as he'd lain beneath her last night in the forest sharpened that ache to a fine edge.

Then he braced his arm around her waist and bent her forward enough so he could slide his hand between them. Suddenly, he probed her bottom with those soapy strokes, his broad hand parting her cheeks intimately. Rising up on tiptoes to manage his access, she didn't accomplish any more than to invite him to explore further…

"Anthony!" The man touched her in places he had no business touching, whether under the pretense of cleansing or not.

"Shh," he murmured thickly and hung on tight, not curbing his exploration with those soapy fingers one bit.

To Tess's amazement, she found herself not wanting to pull away as much as rock her hips to ride the sensation.

Who knew *that* would feel so good?

But feel good it did. So good, in fact, that she would have fallen on her face had he not held her so tight, each soapy stroke creating just enough pressure to make her start vibrating from the inside out.

Her sex clenched hotly, needily, and she wanted to swing around in his arms and hop on for a hard ride.

But Anthony had other plans.

He caught a nipple and gave a squeeze. The pleasure rode through her like a wave, hot and powerful and intense.

He laughed, and some dim part of her barely functioning brain recognized that he must have expected her reaction because he caught her easily when she swayed.

No one man should have such power over her.

No man ever had.

But these were thoughts that Tess couldn't reason through right now, not when she found herself held securely in his strong arms then led to the bench.

She stretched out, testing the strength of languid muscles, treating him to the sight of her spread out naked and clean. She had no idea what Anthony had planned next, but she sincerely hoped it involved his mouth.

Just the memory of the way he'd pleasured her with his mouth last night excited her. But he didn't even glance her way, instead heading to the valet on one of the shower walls to return with…

A razor?

She frowned when he handed her a small mirror.

"Will you hold this? I need to shave."

"I didn't mind your stubbly cheeks between my thighs last night. Hint, hint."

He flashed that lethal grin, and her insides melted.

"My turn tonight, Tess."

"Really?"

He nodded. "You had your way with me last night. It's only fair to return the favor."

She couldn't argue that. He had very graciously let her lead, even though she knew he'd been itching to impress her. And he *had* impressed her—by putting aside his wants for hers.

And taking her apart at the seams anyway.

She wouldn't admit *that*, though, so when he sank onto the floor beside her, she just positioned the mirror.

She found the sight of him dragging that razor over his stubbly cheeks arousing. Tess couldn't explain why. True, he was a beautiful man. His hair, wet and slick, clung to his neck and shoulders, a sexy look that made him seem bad boy in the extreme despite the green foam slathered along his jaw and neck.

He arched a brow. "Am I boring you, *chère?*"

"Not at all."

The companionable silence fell between them again, and Tess marveled at how easily they spent time together. Here they were butt naked with barely a week's acquaintance and one night of intimacy between them. Perhaps because they were spending around-the-clock time together. Three days in a car, and they had no choice but to get close. She couldn't make a ladies' room run without him knowing about it. Still, she couldn't recall this feeling with any other man she'd dated.

His cheeks had a slightly raw look to them when he finished, and he plucked away the mirror with a "thanks" and rinsed his face beneath a jet.

Then returned with the razor.

"Miss a spot?" she asked, trying to talk herself into rolling off this bench so she could rinse the conditioner from her hair and dry off.

That big cushy bed called to her. She wanted to slide between the sheets with a clean naked man.

"Mmm-hmm."

She peered curiously at his face, but couldn't see anything but kissable skin. "Looks good to me."

"The missing spot is on you."

"Where?" She lifted a leg in the air and ran a hand down her calf. Her skin felt baby-buns smooth.

"Not your legs. Here." He knelt beside her and smoothed his palm along her sex.

"You like bald women?" She wasn't sure what to make of this.

He grimaced. "Not *bald,* but I want you ultrasensitive. I want you to feel everything I plan to do to you tonight."

"Will it involve your mouth?"

"Mmm-hmm. You seemed to enjoy yourself last night."

Boy, had she ever. She wasn't about to admit that to Mr. I-Want-You-To-Feel-Everything over there, so she just spread her legs in an invitation.

If it involved his mouth, she'd be happy to oblige him.

Sinking onto the bench, he positioned himself between her spread legs in a breathtaking display of shifting muscle and squeaky-clean skin. "Sure you don't mind?"

"I'll let you know when it starts growing back."

With a laugh, he speared his fingers into the trimmed tuft of curls at the juncture of her thighs and gave a tug.

Tess swallowed back a moan. How much more sensitive could she possibly get?

When he shot a blob of shaving gel between her thighs, she knew she'd find out soon enough. And she didn't mind a bit. The sight of his dark hands working the gel to a lather made her sex give a slow squeeze. Especially when he started up all this perfunctory touching and tugging to manage a clean shave with a disposable razor. A very neat trick. And *arousing.*

"Wow. The razor has never felt like this the million or so times I've shaved my legs."

"That's because I'm doing the honors."

"And you do them very well. *Too* well. I don't think I believe what you told me about bald women."

He didn't answer right away, too occupied with working his way down that sensitive place where her thigh met all her private places. Slipping his fingers along her sex, he caught her curls and separated her sensitive folds so she could feel the steamy air everywhere.

Her stomach contracted. Her thighs quivered.

Anthony smiled, clearly liking her reaction.

"It's not about hair, *chère.* It's about touch. I want you to feel me when I touch you, with nothing in the way."

Pleasure turned his voice whiskey smooth, a sound that rippled through her senses, drugged her with its potency. He thumbed the tiny knot that made her pleasure simmer. "Just think about how good this'll feel when my mouth is on you."

That thought alone would have made her sigh, even if Anthony hadn't been idly thumbing her through the slick passage of shaving gel.

"Can't wait," she admitted.

"Me, either."

Tess liked that Anthony shared his passion so easily, liked how she felt so sexy and aroused and comfortable in the face of his passion.

"You know what I like about us?"

"What's that?" he asked absently.

"It's easy being together."

Her admission hadn't sounded nearly so intimate in her mind as it did aloud, and when Anthony stopped in midstroke to gaze at her curiously, Tess hoped she hadn't made one of the dating gaffes she'd read about in *Metropolitan,* the magazine for modern single women.

But Anthony didn't shy away from her honesty. He looked thoughtful when he met her gaze. "Me, too, *chère*. Me, too."

Somehow his admission sounded equally intimate, and Tess was amazed at how quickly she'd managed to take a casual, comfortable moment and turn it into something more.

Why had she felt the need to?

This question had no place between them. They were all about the here and now, about *fun,* about a break from reality. All too soon their little vacation would be over, and she'd be introducing him to her daddy for business.

She needed to remember that.

"Come with me," he finally said. "I want to clean you up."

Tess let him lead her back under the jets, glad for the distraction. She didn't want to think right now. Not when he worked his soapy hands over her body. Not when he helped her rinse the conditioner from her hair with that hungry gleam in his eyes.

"Stay under the water until I grab some towels."

Tess watched him slip out of the shower, wasn't entirely sure what to make of the way she felt right now.

She stubbornly shoved aside her thoughts, and when Anthony returned with warm towels, she moved into his arms, so their bodies met in a melding of wet skin and sensitive body parts.

To her pleasure, Anthony couldn't resist touching her at such close range, and for every part she managed to dry on him, she found herself dodging his caresses, being aroused by his laughter, being made love to with those bedroom glances.

To touch and be touched.

And then it was her turn.

He grazed the warm towel easily over her, polishing the water from her skin in almost gentle strokes. He massaged her shoulders, her arms, then carefully dried each finger before working his way down her front.

Anthony didn't talk, and she found she didn't have anything to say, either. That companionable silence had fallen again while the moment was charged with awareness, and promise.

When he sank to his knees before her, patting dry her newly shaved sex with soft touches, Tess realized that he hadn't been kidding when he'd said *ultra* sensitive. She wound up spearing her fingers into his wet hair to hang on, liking the way his wet waves felt beneath her fingers. His hair might look rebellious, but it felt decadent. This man was all about pleasure, and she enjoyed something as simple as his untrimmed hair.

After dropping the towels beside the sink, he grabbed her makeup bag. "Is your comb in here?"

She nodded, reaching out to dig through the bag when he opened it, their fingers brushing. Anthony slid his fingers through hers, an oh-so-simple handhold that somehow took on crazy new significance when he didn't let go.

After returning her bag to the vanity, he snagged a bottle of body lotion along with the comb, led her toward the bed then sat on the edge. He pulled her between his spread legs. She knew he only meant to comb her hair, but like holding hands, his attention suddenly felt like so much more.

Arousing. Exciting. *Overwhelming.*

What was it about his strong thighs anchoring her securely or the almost-erection pressed against her back that made her feel as if more than fun was happening between them? They were enjoying a thrill in an expensive hotel room while they raced to the coast. She shouldn't be wondering why he'd been so handy with the razor between her thighs.

But she was very interested in the women he'd honed his shaving skills on, which made no sense whatsoever. Tess had seen his résumé, knew he was several years older than she was. Had she honestly expected such an attractive, charming man to stay hidden in his New Orleans garage all the time?

Of course not. So why was she suddenly wondering where she ranked with the women he'd dated?

9

CLOSING HER EYES as he worked the comb through her hair, Tess shut out all stimuli and mentally cautioned herself against wandering thoughts. She'd signed on for a race to the coast.

She'd signed on for fun.

That's exactly what she planned to have.

Scooting forward, she escaped his warm embrace. He reached out to catch her, but she stepped away, shaking out her hair, letting the wet strands play over her shoulders, a chilly reminder that she needed to stay in control.

But Anthony wasn't having any part of her escape. Almost before she realized he'd moved, he'd slipped his foot between her legs and tossed her off balance. He stood before she could brace herself then, in a blur of motion, he spun her around and hoisted her up.

She barely had a chance to gasp before finding herself looking up at him from the middle of the bed.

For a breathless moment, Tess could only stare. By then he'd straddled her in another impossibly fast move.

"My way tonight, *chère*."

There was no doubt he meant what he said, but she didn't miss the amusement underlying his expression, just enough to spark her bravado.

"What was *that?*"

"Just making sure I get equal time."

Not much of a question anymore, as he had her pinned to the bed. "No, I meant what was *that?* It was some sort of move…or something. Do you work out?"

That was a stupid question. The man wouldn't have his body without working out. Add in his look of pure male satisfaction… He clearly liked that he'd surprised her.

"Martial arts."

"Oh." She should have guessed. No one moved as he had without lots of practice.

"Do you know what I like about you, Tess?"

"What's that?"

"You're a woman who knows what you want, and you're not afraid to take it."

"What do you think I want?"

"Me."

One word issued in that lazy bayou voice made goose bumps spray over her skin. One word that was oh-so true.

Tess did want him, so much that she liked how her world narrowed down to the sight of his dashing smile and broad shoulders when she lay underneath him. She liked the way he held her pinned to the bed with his strong thighs and very obvious proof of his desire.

She liked that he wanted her, liked it much more than she ever would have guessed.

"You know what I like about us?" he asked, his voice gentling, or maybe that was just the way his golden-brown eyes melted over her.

"What?"

"We're good together."

That intimacy thing was happening again, a feeling that

hinted more than fun was happening here. A feeling that made her want to slip her arms around his neck and hold him close.

Tess wasn't at all sure why she felt so tender and dreamy tonight, but sex seemed to make her wax romantic. She didn't bother resisting. Looping her arms around his neck, she pressed up against him, indulging the unfamiliar feeling, even though she wasn't a woman who usually looked for tender moments.

Anthony seemed to be a man who liked them, though. He nestled her close, blocked out her view of the world with his big warm body then rested his chin in the crook of her neck. He seemed content to hold her with his cheek pressed to hers, the silence filled with only the hush of their breathing and the awareness of how well their bodies fit together.

She had no idea how much time had passed before he said, "Hang on," and tightened his grip around her. With a series of small moves, he maneuvered them around on the bed.

"Anthony!" Tess couldn't help laughing. All his hard muscles rode her in all the right places—places that flared to life with desire, places that tickled. "What are you doing?"

"Getting you where I want you." He inched them forward until her head hit the pillows.

"I'd move if you asked."

"I don't want to let go. You feel too good."

So did he, but she felt a zip of pure feminine satisfaction to hear him admit it.

"You know what I like about you, Anthony?"

"What's that, *chère?*"

"You don't pull any punches. You're up-front about how you feel."

"I feel…" His voice trailed off as he braced himself one-handed and started propping pillows behind her. "How's that?"

"Comfy." She felt like a princess perched on a cushy throne and decided she liked the feeling. "You feel what?"

He raked a lazy gaze over her, a smile touching the corners of his mouth and making her feel so beautiful.

"I feel like touching you." He reached for the lotion, warmed a dollop in his hands.

"Oh, I think I'm going to like this."

He dragged his palm down her throat. "Oh, you will. I promise. It's my turn to impress you tonight, remember?"

Suddenly, his hands were everywhere, and Tess wasn't as much impressed as she was overwhelmed by sensation. His hands worked the lotion into her skin in firm strokes. Not so much a massage as an exploration of her body. Every touch designed to bring pleasure. Heat began to pour through her, a languid sensation that made her skin tingle and her blood simmer.

His strong fingers worked the muscles in her arms until she felt boneless. He pressed kisses to each of her fingertips, gentle grazes of his lips against skin she hadn't realized could be so sensitive. He'd told her romance was an Italian thing, and while lying propped against the pillows, feeling decadent and indulged, Tess agreed.

He was a very romantic man. Determined, too, because every time she reached for him, wanting to touch, to participate, to return some of the pleasure, she provoked another assault.

And when he scooted down the length of her body,

muscles trailing over skin he'd caressed into aching awareness, and settled himself between her legs, she knew what
was coming next...*his mouth.*

She sighed. Her body shot from drowsy to excited in a
heartbeat, some part of her not believing the way he'd
made her feel last night had been real. Surely all those exquisite orgasms had been some trick of her imagination.

But when he brushed his fingers over her newly shaved
sex, worked the lotion in with deliberate thoroughness,
Tess knew she hadn't imagined anything about last night.

Even the sight of him aroused her.

The lines of his long body stretched out before her, a
gorgeous display of golden skin and sculpted curves. Just
trailing her gaze over his broad back, trim waist and tight
butt felt like an indulgence, a gorging of her senses. He had
great legs, too, more hard muscle with that light sprinkling
of tawny hair. Even his feet were tanned and good-looking.

Who'd ever heard of good-looking *feet?*

Tess buried herself back against the pillows, deciding
she had it bad for this man. And it was no wonder, either.
Anthony DiLeo was too hot for her own good.

What woman could resist the way he slid his hands
down her thighs, coaxed her bended knees to cradle his
wide shoulders in an incredibly erotic pose? And when he
shot her a roguish smile while lowering his face between
her thighs... Her breath caught and held as he settled in,
and she felt the first warm drag of his tongue along her
most private places.

Pleasure seized every muscle between her knees and her
throat, and heat radiated outward from the point of contact. Her memory had been dead-on accurate.

Ohmigosh.

He knew exactly where to breathe those hot bursts of air to prolong the sensation. He nibbled his way into all her private places, tiny nips and bites that warmed her up for what was to come. He knew precisely where to spear his tongue and seek out all those receptive spots that quivered for his attention.

How could she not respond to such a skillful assault? Her breasts grew heavy and tight. It was all she could do to grab the pillows and hang on for the ride.

Anthony wasn't content to do just the mouth thing, either. He involved his hands in the game, calloused fingertips probing skin around that oh-so-sensitive knot of nerve endings, a touch that made her tremble.

And when he freed that tiny place, drew it inside his warm mouth in a slow wet pull…

"Oh!" She exhaled the sound on a sigh that echoed through the quiet room.

He was pleased with her response, pleased he had her hanging on to the pillows for dear life. She could feel his smile against all her skin when he raised his gaze, pleasure dancing in his eyes.

And when he used his fingers to test her moist opening…just enough pressure to make her want more…just enough to make her arch her hips and create more friction, she wished he had six hands so he could touch her everywhere. Her breasts ached so much….

Releasing the pillow, she reached for him, brushed her fingers over his shoulder, down that hunky bicep until she could catch a good hold.

"Anthony, up here." She barely recognized her own voice as it rasped through the quiet.

He let her guide his arm up, up, up…then he took things from there. He splayed his big hand over her breast, cupping her fullness as she arched up into his touch. He even did her one better. Slithering his other hand out from beneath her, he handled her other one, too, kneading, arousing.

He caught her nipples and rolled them hard, making her gasp out as sensation jammed through her. And through it all he just kept sucking at his maddeningly slow and steady pace. He sensed her pleasure building, but he wouldn't let her rush, even though she could feel him everywhere, couldn't stop rocking her hips.

And she wasn't the only one feeling. Anthony groaned, and he ground his erection into the mattress.

Suddenly Tess was done playing—she wanted to feel him inside her. Reaching for him, she sank her fingers into those broad shoulders, urged him to move up into her arms.

But he resisted and his earlier words echoed in her memory. *"My way tonight, chère."*

His way would likely kill her, but she knew their time together was too sweet to rush. He was right about that. But she wanted…oh, how she wanted. When he stopped sucking to tongue her with hot wet strokes, she almost bolted off the bed.

Those hands on her breasts stopped her, though, and he gave a breathy chuckle against her sex, another sensation that made her writhe. He lifted his face and met her gaze above the freshly shaved mound.

"See what I meant about ultrasensitive?" His sexy mouth gleamed with her body's moisture, and her sex gave a hard throb at the sight.

"Oh, yeah," was all she managed to get out in a gravelly voice that made him smile.

Then he brought one hand down and wriggled his finger into all her damp heat. "Like that?"

"Oh, Anthony." She couldn't stop rocking her hips and rode that stroke with a long, slow thrust.

Mmm, mmm, mmm, mmm, mmm.

"What about this?" Slipping another finger backward, he ventured off into places that awoke some naggy little part of her brain with a demand to stop. But for the life of her, Tess couldn't think why. Pleasure overruled naggy doubts and any ability to think anyway.

Especially when his palm hit her hot spot.

Then she was powerless to do anything but clutch his shoulders and ride that pressure.

When it broke, it broke *big*, overheating every nerve until she shook unceremoniously and collapsed against the pillows. She heaved broken breaths as though she'd just run a race and finally opened her eyes to the sight of utter satisfaction on Anthony's handsome face.

"Impressed yet?" he asked conversationally.

"That mouth of yours should be registered." She panted out the words. "You killed me. Happy now?"

"You're not dead, *chère*."

And to prove it, he pressed his palm against her hot spot again, made her tremble as if she'd been struck by lightning.

"See. Everything's still working."

"*Hmph.*" Flinging her arm over her head, she exhaled deeply, let her eyes drift closed again.

Anthony maneuvered around until he lay against her. She wanted to wrap herself around him, hold him close, but couldn't break through her lethargy long enough to lift an arm to flop it across him. But when he began idly thumbing her breast, she did manage to crack an eyelid to stare.

"What?" Laughter sparkled in those bedroom eyes. "You thought we were done?"

She couldn't have replied if she'd had the strength to open her mouth. She didn't. Turned out the man wasn't interested in talking anyway. He coaxed her onto her tummy. Then he started massaging warm lotion into her skin, along her thighs, her butt, her waist.

While working his way up her back, he nestled his erection cozily against her bottom. To Tess's amazement, she felt life signs in places that, by all rights, should have been dead. But there was something about the way she felt right now, something she couldn't put a name to, something that felt more than boneless and replete.

Her senses sharpened in on Anthony now, on the feel of his hands moving over her skin. Desire pooled low in her tummy, and her sex gave the odd clench, remnants of that incredible orgasm.

Her body had become a finely tuned instrument of pleasure, her every response honing in on his touches. It went beyond wanting him, beyond the incredible way he made her feel. She wanted to make him feel, too. To make him melt into a puddle of firing impulses the way she had.

To Tess's surprise, she wasn't as boneless as she'd thought. Either Anthony's hands had infused her with energy or he inspired her to new boldness because right now she knew exactly what she wanted.

Lifting her hips, she wedged that impressive erection snugly between her cheeks. Then she rode his length with a rather neat rolling motion that dragged warm skin against hot male heat. He groaned softly, and she rode him again, another slow deliberate stroke designed to get a response.

He responded. "Ah, *chère,* you feel so good."

His arms came around her. He slid his hands along the length of her arms, twined their fingers together. Pressing his cheek to hers, he covered her with his big body, such an intimate position as she mimed the act of lovemaking with her rocking hips. His erection swelled eagerly.

Tess felt eager, too. Excitement reawakened with a vengeance. A feeling so completely easy and natural that she'd never known the like. A feeling as if her pleasure hinged upon his, and the most important thing in the world she could do was coax another raw groan from his mouth.

She was back to his mouth again.

And there it was, close enough to kiss. She pressed her lips there, half kisses, just tastes really, because that's all she could reach. But even such simple touches were exquisitely erotic, supremely intimate. Their breaths twisted and lingered around each other. Their bodies swayed together sensually.

His throaty growl burst against her lips. A tremor ran through him, and she wasn't surprised when he lifted his hips, a huge move that freed his erection to slip between her thighs. All she had to do was arch her bottom in invitation.

He nipped her mouth with biting kisses. His fingers clung to hers, keeping her body stretched full beneath him as he shifted, took aim and slid inside her.

Tess stretched to accommodate him, her body slick, welcoming. Sighs tumbled from her lips, and she clung to his hands, an anchor as their bodies came together all white heat and desire. She felt surrounded by him, by the fingers that held her steady, by the solid heaviness of his beautiful body, by the overwhelming heat he pressed deep inside.

His thighs flexed, and he rode her with long, slow thrusts. She rose to meet each stroke, her hips the only part of her body she could move to create a sultry ebb and flow as they rocked together. A pace that blocked out the rest of the world, chased away all thoughts except the way pleasure built, intense, inevitable. A slow rise of tension that grew so great, so overwhelming, Tess let go completely.

She lost herself in the sounds of his quickened breaths as he reached the edge and his thrusts pushed her over, too, the pleasure shattering in another blinding orgasm that she knew instinctively she could only experience with this man.

Only Anthony.

10

"WHAT'S ON YOUR MIND?" Anthony reached for his sunglasses to shield his gaze from the glaring sun. "You've been staring out that window for twenty miles. Thinking about Tori Grant's article?"

Tess glanced his way, a smile on her lips. "No. Although I thought she did a nice job with it."

"Thinking about your father's phone call?"

"No, he sounded better since Glen was able to bump up the alert status with the Post Office."

"Were you thinking about how impressed you are with me, *chère?*"

She smiled. "As a matter of fact, I was. I'm not so ready to head back to the real world yet. I'd like to relax in San Francisco before we head home. If we stay in a hotel with decent security, I'm sure Daddy won't grouse. What do you think?"

Anthony thought he'd done exactly what he'd set out to do—impress Tess. It was all over her from the way she'd slept wrapped around him last night to the contented look on her face right now. He'd impressed her in a way he hadn't intended, of course, because seduction had been the last thing on his mind when he'd shown up at the convention.

Shifting his gaze back to Tess, he watched as she snuggled back into the corner between her door and seat, knees drawn up, silky dark head resting against the window, seat belt stretched impossibly across her. She wrapped her hands around her cup of Starbucks coffee and sipped contentedly.

Anthony wished he felt as content as she looked.

He'd held her close last night, and for the few hours they hadn't made love, he'd tried to sleep. He *should* have slept. He was beyond tired—the sex *should* have pushed him over the edge.

But the sex had pushed his *head* over the edge.

All night long his brain had been in overdrive. Reliving past mistakes. Tormenting himself with the way his life might have turned out if he hadn't been so caught up in proving himself. How he must not have learned much from his mistakes because here he was with a special woman who did things to him that hadn't been done in forever and his work was square in the middle of them.

Sometime during the past two nights of incredible sex, things had taken a turn he hadn't foreseen.

They'd gotten *complicated.*

Anthony had started this venture wanting an introduction, now he wanted more than a few extra days before they headed back to the real world.

He had no damn business wanting anything else. Tess had made it loud and clear from the start that she had no use for men who used her to get to her father. She thought of him as a fling with a capital *F* with no possibility of anything else.

Anthony found he wasn't content being her road rally entertainment, not one damn bit.

"I'm the Anthony DiLeo in Anthony DiLeo Automotive," he finally said. "Taking a few extra days isn't a problem, as long as I'm back in New Orleans by the sixteenth."

"You're sure?"

"Positive." He needed to figure out what he wanted from this woman and how to get it.

A few extra days together was at least a place to start.

"I DON'T KNOW WHY they bother calling this a race," Anthony said from the passenger's seat as he tried to read the San Francisco street map in the dark. "We didn't get on the road until noon."

Personally, Tess had enjoyed sleeping in and the break from the early-morning rally routine, but it had been a long day and they were on the final stretch to the last checkpoint. "I told you it's a symbolic race. Whoever comes in first gets the honor of turning over all the proceeds to the Women's Cancer League."

"If tonight's the punch line, then why did we sit through that boring-as-hell ceremony this morning?"

Tess smiled. "That boring-as-hell ceremony was supposed to be *fun*. Didn't you hear people laughing?"

"Oh, that's right. The souvenirs we've been picking up," he said dryly. "How could I have forgotten? Keene Motors' bobble-head cow from Amarillo had me in tears."

"Ha, ha. Everyone liked our slot machine from the Parisian, though. That was really sweet of Tori's husband to make it a gift." This cranky man needed some sleep. He didn't know it yet but they were going to find a hotel somewhere on the water tonight. He'd get all the sleep he needed, and then some. "That boring-as-hell ceremony breaks up the schedule. If you haven't figured it out yet, the checkpoints have been roughly six hundred miles apart. That makes for a decent driving day. But if we'd left at the normal time today, we'd have arrived in San Francisco during traffic hour. After four days on the road, no one wants to battle rush-hour traffic, so the committee lets us sleep late and start late on the last day so we don't get in until after dark."

Anthony just grunted, but Tess was pleased. They were making really decent time. It was just after nine o'clock and if their route through the city proved as easy as the rest of the day, they'd be in good shape.

They fell back into silence as Tess wound through the city streets with Anthony's direction. The night-dark city unfolded around them, and she enjoyed her rising excitement as they neared the end of the rally and a few more days together, *alone.*

It wasn't until they passed a gas station for the second time that Tess realized they must have driven in a circle.

"Are we lost, Anthony?"

"No."

"Are you sure? I think we drove past that gas station already." She shifted her gaze off the road, and one glance at Anthony was enough to make her cold. "What's wrong?"

"I don't want you to freak, *chère,* but we've got a little problem."

"What?"

"Someone's been following us for the past dozen blocks. An SUV filled with thugs. I can't tell how old they are, but they're not kids."

Lubbock might not be the biggest city in Texas, but Tess knew enough about big cities to know trouble happened a lot more often when the population got high and tight. She hoped trouble hadn't latched onto her and Anthony. "What should we do?"

"I had you make a turn back there so they'd think we were lost, but if you put those skills you learned with the Maverick to work, we might shake them."

Tess nodded and tightened her grip on the wheel.

They were silent as Anthony navigated her through a series of quick turns that took them off their declared route to the checkpoint still across the city. She resisted the urge to look in the rearview mirror and just kept her eyes on the dark streets. It was night, and a pedestrian could all too easily step out from between parked cars.

She could only go so fast without getting dangerous, and she pushed that limit to the max.

"No good," he finally said. "They know we're onto them. They're closing the distance."

"Is it a gang?"

"I thought so at first, but they're on us like glue. I don't get the feeling this is random."

She didn't like that *something* she heard in his voice, the inevitability, and when he unfastened his seat belt and twisted around to reach into the back seat, his intensity made adrenaline pump so fast she had to swallow a lump in her throat.

"Don't worry, *chère*. They've probably just taken a liking to your Gremlin."

She gave a short laugh despite herself, appreciated his effort to make her feel better. She watched in her periphery as he kneeled beside her to stretch all the way to the hatch.

"What are you doing?"

"Grabbing something from your trunk."

She would have asked what, but she had to do some fancy driving to miss a car pulling away from the curb. She needed to keep her attention on this road. Cruising along these narrow streets so far over the speed limit was begging for trouble.

Anthony settled back in beside her with a tire iron in hand, and Tess tried to stave off a rising sense of premonition as he flipped open his phone and made a call.

He summed up the situation, and she knew he'd called 9-1-1.

She finally glanced in the rearview mirror. "They're getting closer, Anthony. Do you want me to speed up?"

He shook his head. His voice was calm when he said, "Did you notice that last street sign by any chance?"

"No."

"We're from out of town." He spoke into the phone. "We got off our route trying to shake these guys, so I don't have a cross street yet."

He listed a few landmarks as they drove past them, then Tess's headlights reflected off a street sign as she eased up on the pedal to cruise through an intersection.

"That sign says Tavist Avenue."

Anthony repeated the information. "We'll try to keep heading west, but we're driving a purple Gremlin with a white racing stripe and Texas tags. Tell the patrol they couldn't miss us if they tried."

Tess gave a huff, a crazy sound that had only the barest trace of bravado.

The traffic light ahead switched to yellow.

"Run it," Anthony said coolly, with the phone still poised at his ear.

Tess hit the gas and leaned on the horn to signal traffic, but just as she hit the intersection, the car idling on the north side of the street jumped the light.

"Damn it." She swerved hard to avoid a collision, forced to brake as her trajectory changed, and she was suddenly facing a line of parked cars.

Wheeling the car around, she narrowly cleared an old sedan's fender.

But those seconds cost her big.

She came out of the spin to find the SUV screeching toward her, cutting off her escape. Tess had to brake to renegotiate her direction before she gunned the engine again.

The SUV looked like a monster bearing down on them, and when it nailed her quarter panel, she had to brake again.

This time the SUV's doors swung wide and men jumped out.

Six men wearing ski masks.

Panic drowned out the sound of Anthony's voice as she threw the car into Reverse, spun the wheel and shimmied out of the crush, scraping the SUV's fender in the process.

The big vehicle bucked when it came up against her sturdy Gremlin, and Tess almost had them clear when she heard the shots. Two loud cracks in the night. The wheel jerked in her hands. One—or was it two?—tires blew. She hung on and braked hard to change direction again, but this time the stop cost.

Men swarmed them, men who didn't look like any gang members she'd ever seen on the news.

"Keep the doors locked and stay inside." Anthony flung his door wide, jumped out and slammed it shut behind him.

"Anthony!"

He was gone. The solid *thunk* of the closing door jump-started her heart again, helped her think through panic.

Slamming the lock button down, Tess grabbed his cell phone off the seat to hear the woman on the other end trying to urge her onto the line. Tess shouted, "Send the police" into the receiver as she yanked open her glove compartment. Damn man. He was one to six out there. And they had guns.

Digging for her pepper spray, she grabbed the canister just as her driver's window exploded.

Tess had all she could do to scramble away from the narrow wooden club that suddenly appeared. Cold chunks of shattered glass bounced off her cheek and head before she brought her arm up to protect her face. She dropped the phone.

Rough laughter exploded outside, muffled thumps that might have been someone hitting the ground. Anthony? More shattered glass as the club cleared away debris. She thumbed off the pepper spray's safety while scooting farther toward the passenger's seat.

A black-clad arm shot through the broken window. A strong hand latched onto her forearm like a vice. Tess allowed herself to be pulled upright just enough to catch sight of the hooded face… She shot the pepper spray.

Some of the blast must have made it through the holes in the ski mask because the man's grip slackened. He reared back, whacking his head on the doorjamb with a solid crack. In that split instant, Tess repositioned herself so when he came back at her she could defend herself.

She planted her heel in his face and earned a muttered curse. Kicking again and again, she dodged his attempts to grab her, clutching the canister in case he caught her. She couldn't see the phone, couldn't spare a glance to find it.

Finally, his fingers bit into her ankle, and she clawed at the door, resisted by grabbing the handle and hanging on. She kicked hard with her other foot, trying to break his hold.

Strength won out, breaking her grip on the handle just as the passenger's window exploded above her head. She spat away tiny chunks of broken glass that clung to her lips, crying out when the attacker at her feet jerked her sharply toward him.

He fumbled one-handed with the lock. With her leg bent at an odd angle halfway through the window, all she could do was clutch the steering wheel to resist. She gritted her teeth against a blast of pain as he pulled open the door and broken glass caught her calf.

Tess knew he meant to pull her through next, and she managed to lock her arm in the cage of the steering wheel and get some weight behind it.

She leaned on the horn.

The blast of sound shrieked through the night reassuringly solid and loud, and she had the wild thought that no late model car had a horn that could come close to competing with those made in the seventies.

She leaned on that horn again, and again.

"Stop the bitch." A harsh command was growled out.

Tess clung to the steering wheel with steel in her arm, managing to break his grip. She bucked and kicked so her attacker couldn't grab her again.

Out of nowhere, a bat slammed into the windshield, hard enough to depress and web the tempered glass. Within seconds, the hatch window exploded, raining glass into the front seat.

She didn't know why these men were vandalizing her car, could only cling to the wheel, ram her fist into the horn, and keep kicking out at her attacker.

Then hands reached in from the passenger side for a fistful of hair. Her head snapped back painfully, and she cried out, giving way to the pressure before it ripped her hair out by the root.

"Get her." A rough voice broke over her head.

The attacker at her feet yanked the door completely open and the lower half of her spilled to the ground.

He was on her in an instant. She couldn't disentangle her hand from the steering wheel quickly enough, and felt her wrist snap as she was dragged off the seat.

The keening horn faded to silence. For a stunned instant, Tess could only absorb the shock of the pain, the blood throbbing so hard in her ears, she thought she'd be sick.

Another powerful pull, and she slithered off the seat, striking her head on the floorboard on her way down. White light exploded behind her lids, but cleared in time for her to see him rise above her…. With her undamaged hand, she sprayed another blast of pepper spray.

He roared a curse and staggered backward, giving her a chance to roll free. Cradling her injured wrist against her chest, her skin slick from sweat, Tess let adrenaline fuel her across the pavement. When she cleared her fender, she saw what was happening in the street, and her heartbeat stalled.

The ski-masked men huddled around Anthony.

Another man joined them, swinging his way through

the group with that wicked bat, but Anthony halted a blow with the tire iron, sending the bat spinning from his attacker's hands. Another lunged. Anthony staggered, rolling onto his back and bringing the man down with him.

It took Tess a second to recognize that while he might be fighting too many men, he wasn't struggling. He was a blur of skilled motion, striking out at one after another. He wielded that tire iron, blocking a blow then smashing it into the face of another, knocking him momentarily out of the fight.

She could only stare as he launched himself onto one of the attackers in a move she'd only seen in the movies. He came down on top of the man, landed a solid blow with his fist, then rolled away leaving the guy sprawled motionless on the ground.

But Tess stared a minute too long and forgot her own attacker. He'd recovered and launched himself on top of her, pinning her to the pavement. Her injured hand caught underneath her and a volley of pain was the last thing she knew.

ANTHONY COULDN'T GET TO Tess. Every time he fought off one thug, another had to be dealt with. But he'd heard her cry and couldn't look to see if she was all right. He couldn't lose his concentration, not with her safety in the balance.

These were no ordinary thugs—they were thugs with some skill, which meant they had money behind them. Not enough skill to take him down, but enough that if he screwed up, they'd overpower him by their sheer numbers.

He wouldn't screw up.

Nailing the back of some guy's head, he felt the tire iron vibrate as it struck a blow that took another thug out.

He wouldn't screw up.

The fifth one rejoined them, which meant Tess only had to contend with one. Not the one with the gun. That one he'd been keeping busy so he didn't have a chance to retrieve the weapon Anthony had kicked out of his hand. It had skittered beneath a parked car, and he needed to get it first to end this fight.

Blocking a blow with a bat, he found himself restrained as the thug with the silver eyebrow studs grabbed him around the throat. Silver Stud must have thought he had the upper hand because he didn't press his advantage.

Mistake.

Anthony drove the tire iron backward, catching him in the stomach. The force of the blow sent him reeling backward, and Anthony broke free. He dropped to the ground and rolled toward the car. If the gun hadn't flown too far underneath…

"Assholes," someone yelled from a window over a shop. "I'm calling the cops."

Thank you.

Tess's quick thinking with the car horn had called attention to them, and that yell bought Anthony the few precious seconds he needed to stretch his arm beneath the car, feeling the concrete beneath his splayed fingers, searching….

A kick to his back knocked the breath from his lungs. Before he could maneuver around to gain his feet, the bat caught the side of his face a stunning blow.

His head exploded and it was all he could do to shake off the sudden daze. He didn't resist when violent hands dragged him to his feet. He didn't do anything as one of the thugs held him by the throat and the others gathered around to kick his ass.

Then Anthony leveled the automatic pistol at one of the approaching thug's legs, fired, then brought the weapon back to rest against the cheek of the guy who held him.

He heard a sharp intake of breath, and nudged the gun in a silent demand. "Let go."

The arm around his throat eased off. Without moving the gun, Anthony spun and caught the thug around the neck. Shielding himself behind the guy, he said, "Call off your friends."

The sight of his buddy on the ground clutching his bleeding knee seemed to be all the incentive this one needed.

"Back off," he yelled.

The one standing closest took a step backward. The one beside Tess bolted behind a parked car, safely out of Anthony's line of fire. He held the gun steady and took in the scene in a glance. Two on the ground disabled. One injured. One gone.

And Tess sprawled beside the Gremlin, unmoving.

"Get against the car." Anthony struggled against a surge of red heat, a need to fire this gun and end this fight so he could get to Tess. "Hands where I can see them. Now start talking or I start pulling this trigger. Who sent you?"

He barely noticed the sirens as police cruisers surrounded the intersection or the visibars that flashed in the darkness.

11.

"WE HAVE YOUR STATEMENT, and we'll be in touch," the detective told Anthony. "Don't worry. Once we get those guys booked, I'm sure they'll start talking."

"You'll tow the car to your impound lot until I can make arrangements to get it home?"

The man handed him a business card. "It's already there. Call and talk to Jerry when you're squared. Now go see your lady and be glad you made out as well as you did tonight."

Anthony was glad, but when he arrived inside the emergency room to find Tess still unconscious, he didn't feel as though they'd made out well at all.

His chest constricted around a breath as he took in the glossy dark hair tangled around her head, such a stark contrast to the linens on the gurney and her too-pale skin. To his relief, her beautiful face showed no signs of the attack, but she seemed small lying there...*vulnerable.*

"She'll be fine," an unfamiliar voice said.

Anthony glanced at the doctor. The nurse beside him seemed old enough to have a few years of experience behind her, but this guy didn't look much older than Anthony himself.

"Why's she still out?"

"Shock. That's to be expected with the concussion and arm trauma. I'll keep her here for the rest of the night so we can keep an eye on her."

Anthony's gaze zeroed in on Tess's arm. He hadn't noticed that—the white plaster cast blended in with the sheets.

"Broken?"

The doctor nodded. The nurse whispered something to him and both their gazes riveted onto Anthony's face.

"You need to be x-rayed," the doctor said. "I'll send your friend to a room, so we can take a look at you."

"I'm fine."

"You don't look fine. You need stitches on that cheek, and judging by the swelling, you sustained some head injury, too."

If Anthony was being honest, he didn't feel fine. His head felt ready to explode. The skin on his face felt swollen and tight, and he suspected he might have cracked a rib or two.

He didn't feel like being honest.

"I'm fine," he insisted. "I'll go up with Tess."

The nurse frowned. "If you don't let the doctor stitch that cheek, it'll scar."

He just leveled his gaze at her. She shook her head in disapproval and said, "At least let me clean it."

The doctor handed her antiseptic, and he submitted to her ministrations while waiting for the transportation aide to arrive.

Tess didn't awaken as they wheeled her upstairs to a regular floor, and Anthony paced outside the room as the nurse got her settled. He used the time to make the phone call he'd never expected to make.

Ray Macy picked up on the fourth ring, his voice gravelly with sleep. "Yeah."

"This is Anthony DiLeo, sir. I didn't live up to my end of our deal," he said simply, truthfully. "Tess and I were involved in an attack in San Francisco. She'll be fine, but she got banged around some. The doctor wants to keep her in the hospital for the rest of the night to keep his eye on her. I need you to contact her father and let him know where she is."

To Ray Macy's credit, he handled the news well. Maybe it had to do with a family member in crisis. Anthony knew well enough from his own that when something went wrong, family stuck to the business at hand—fixing the problem. There'd always be time later for guilt and blame, and he appreciated Ray Macy not making him feel any worse than he already did. If that were even possible.

By the time he'd relayed the hospital information and disconnected the call, the floor nurse was exiting Tess's room. Anthony decided that he must look like shit, because she glanced his way and gave directions to the coffeepot in the patient pantry room then told him she'd leave pillows and a blanket so he could get some sleep, too.

Anthony thanked her and headed to the pantry, where he grabbed himself a cup of joe and dialed the number of someone he could count on, someone who, with a P.I. background, could help him figure out what to do to protect Tess.

He wasn't waiting around for the police to get those thugs into lockup. He wanted to know who'd come after them and why.

It might be the dead of night in New Orleans, but a sleep-drugged voice answered on the third ring.

"Anthony."

"Hey, princess. Getting your beauty sleep?"

"You all right?" Alarm sharpened her drowsy tone.

He leaned against the counter, amazed by the relief that swept through him, by how much he'd needed to hear a familiar voice right now. The voice of someone he didn't have to impress or prove himself to, someone who wouldn't ask for explanations the way his family would. He needed to hear *her* voice, and he hadn't known how much until she was on the other end, just *there,* waiting.

"Yeah, I'll live, but I need your help."

"Of course."

Of course.

He could practically see her sitting up in bed to shake off sleep, scowling as she wished for some jet-fuel java to speed the process along. The thought made him feel better, in control.

Just hearing her voice helped him understand that the way he felt right now wasn't about being busted up in a fight. It was about the woman lying inside the hospital room down the hall. He cared, damn it, so much that he was in over his head. He recognized how this felt. He worried about keeping Tess safe, questioned whether he could. She'd already been hurt because he hadn't been able to protect her.

But he felt better talking, so he explained what had been happening with the rally, the letters Big Tex had received, the attack and what he'd learned from their attackers.

Harley listened, occasionally asking questions, annoyed that the police couldn't offer any more. She didn't ask for anything except the necessities about Tess, but she would know that this woman was important enough for him to call her, that he wouldn't trust anyone but Harley to help him protect her.

She'd get the significance of that.

"I'll start the preliminary work just as soon as I make some coffee," she said. "I'll catch a flight to San Francisco in the morning. Hopefully the police won't jerk me around, but it doesn't matter. I need to follow the trail from there before it gets cold and find out who springs these guys from lockup."

"This won't screw things up for next week, will it?"

"If I get tied up, I'll fly back for the day."

"You're sure?"

She gave an exasperated huff that came through loud and clear over two thousand miles of bouncing satellite signals. "Why are you asking me stupid questions at three in the morning when I haven't made coffee yet?"

He smiled. He needed reassurance right now, needed to know she'd help him figure this out.

Of course.

It was that simple.

"You don't let her out of your eyesight, Anthony, and I'll find out what's going on."

"Thanks, princess."

"Take care of you, too. Promise?"

He heard the concern in her voice and for a moment he just absorbed the feeling, drew strength from it. "Promise."

"I'll call." She disconnected, and he stood there, savoring the knowledge that he was no longer alone.

Harley was there as she always was, not only to help him sort out the threat against Tess, but to help him sort out his feelings, feelings that suddenly seemed bigger than he was. When he finally made his way to Tess's room, he closed the door and sank into the chair beside the bed, the weight of the night's events settling on him as if it had been strapped across his back.

The room's only light glowed softly above her head, spilling a muted glow across her face. Her lashes clustered on her cheeks, dark semicircles against her pale skin that drew his attention to the faint smudges beneath her eyes, evidence of too many sleepless nights.

He'd been responsible for that, too.

His gaze traveled to her arm propped gingerly on a pillow, the slim fingers extending beyond the smooth edges, the neat pink nails. That cast symbolized the violence of the night.

So many questions rattled around in his head. About the attack. About Tess. But he wasn't alone. To hell with the stupid police. Harley would help him, leaving him free to take care of the most important thing right now—keeping Tess safe.

Hooking his arms on his knees, Anthony leaned forward, finding the position relieved the pounding pressure in his face. Tess exhaled a restless sigh, and he watched as she turned her head to the side, as if she could sense his presence.

She'd held her own tonight, kept her head and raised the alarm, doing her bit to help when he'd been outmanned in that street, unable to keep all their assailants busy.

What bothered him the most was the thought of her being scared. It was a physical ache that hurt more than potentially cracked ribs, split skin or a bruised face.

He needed to hear her say she'd be okay, needed to see that familiar challenge flare in those big green eyes, a look that said she would take whatever life threw at her and triple it. He needed to see her smile.

That need kept surprising him.

Their attraction had taken him off guard. He hadn't expected to get this sucked into a woman ever again. But as he sat in this hospital room watching her sleep, rehashing the events of the past week, everything about him hurting, Anthony understood what he wanted from her, finally recognized what was happening between them. He'd gotten the one thing he'd never thought he would.

A second chance.

TESS STILL SLEPT when Ray Macy and Big Tex Hardaway arrived shortly before dawn.

Anthony rose to greet them, grateful he'd abandoned attempts to sleep and made for the patient coffeepot long ago.

In his Stetson and hand-tooled boots, Big Tex Hardaway could have walked off a television set, and there was no missing Penny Parker's genius at capturing this man's presence in her advertising campaign. Like his TV alter ego, Big Tex was larger than life, brawny rather than tall, with a strong grip and an easy smile.

Tess looked nothing like her father, except for the flash of challenge in his green eyes. The man's gaze traveled over Tess with a look that hit Anthony as the way every father should look at his daughter.

Adoring, with a little possessive and a lot of smitten thrown into the mix.

Anthony nodded to Ray Macy, expected to feel the weight of the man's stare. After all, he'd promised to care for Tess the last time they'd spoken, and here they were inside a hospital.

To his surprise, he didn't see accusation in Ray Macy's face. "I hear we owe you a thanks."

"We talked to the police and the doctor on our flight in." Big Tex stepped back from the bed. "And I checked out everything I could find out about you."

Anthony appreciated the honesty but wasn't sure how to respond, so he went straight to the heart of matters. "Then you know the attack wasn't random."

"Heard all about it from the police. Also heard you questioned the attackers."

How ironic that after all the effort he'd put forth to get in front of this man, Big Tex's first impression of him would involve a street fight and a gun. "I didn't learn as much as I'd hoped. They were paid to rough up Tess's car and knock her out of the race. According to the ones I talked to, she wasn't supposed to get hurt."

"But you were. The police think that's significant."

Anthony thought so, too. "Someone's trying to make a point, but I couldn't tell you what it is. Forcing Tess out of the race doesn't make sense. It's not like there's any prize money at stake here, and since I've only known her a week, I don't have a clue where I fit in. Obviously, my first concern is her safety, so I called in some private investigator friends of mine. They're with Eastman Investigations out of New Orleans.

"You can check them out. It's a reputable firm that does a lot of work with government agencies." Pulling one of Harley's business cards from his wallet, he handed it to Big Tex. "I know about the letters. Do you think they could be connected?"

"Could be," Big Tex said noncommittally and let his words trail off into a silence that got heavier by the second.

Anthony braced himself. The man's intensity clued him in on what was coming next—an interrogation.

Sure enough, Big Tex looked him dead in the eye and said, "Son, I've got some questions, and I'd like straight answers."

"Shoot, sir."

"Until four days ago, I'd never heard your name. Now, all of a sudden, you're running the rally with my daughter, protecting her from bad guys and concerning yourself with who might be after her. Seems like an awful lot going on since you showed up. Should I be worried about you?"

Anthony knew his answer would lay the whole foundation for his relationship with this man. A week ago, he'd wanted that relationship to be all about business.

Now, a lot more rode on his answer.

"I understand your concern, sir. I'm new to the equation, and it looks like I didn't walk in at the best of times. Ray said as much before the rally. Like I told him then, all I have is my reputation to vouch for me, and my word that my intentions toward Tess are honorable."

Big Tex's expression didn't budge, and Anthony knew this man was no one's fool. He'd cut his way through the ranks to his current success with shrewd business tactics and people savvy. At the moment, he was passing judgment on Anthony.

But he hadn't thrown him out yet. It was a start.

"Penny told us you were chasing Tess around the convention to talk about some sort of business," Ray said. "Care to tell us more about that?"

The moment of truth.

Anthony had yet to bridge the distance between bed buddy and serious contender with Tess. If he explained his

AutoTexCare plan and the reason he'd sought Tess out in the first place, he'd only reinforce her belief he was more interested in her father than he was in her.

On the other hand, if he didn't answer this question and fast, he sensed these two were about to send him packing.

Anthony didn't think he had enough leverage with Tess yet to override a veto from the two most important men in her life. And when he glanced at her as she stirred on the bed, he knew there was only one answer he could give, anyway.

The truth.

"I'd rather not tell you about my business with Tess just yet. It isn't a secret or anything mysterious." He gave a dry laugh. "It's not a big deal at all, really, or it wasn't at first. But now there's a problem she and I need to work out."

"DiLeo, that's convoluted as hell," Ray Macy shot back. "Just answer the damn question."

Anthony shrugged. They'd have to take it or leave it on this. He had something to prove to Tess and that came first. "I wish I had more to vouch for me than my word. I don't."

Ray Macy scowled harder, but Big Tex eyed him levelly and asked, "What problem?"

"I want to keep seeing your daughter after this rally is over, but our business is in the way."

Ray Macy gave a snort of undisguised humor, as if out of anything in the world Anthony could have said he'd picked about the stupidest.

Given the circumstances, Anthony would have to agree.

"Do you think she wants to keep seeing you?" Big Tex asked.

"I do." *If* Tess was willing to give him a chance to prove she'd become a lot more important than his Auto-TexCare plan.

Big Tex stared, gauging his worth, calculating the risks. Anthony could see the moment he'd made his decision, recognized the determination in those strikingly familiar eyes.

"You do have something more than your reputation to vouch for you. Your actions. You protected my little girl last night, and from the looks of you that took some doing. Keep your secret for now and work out your problem." He extended his hand. "Don't do me wrong, son. You'll regret it."

Big Tex had a father's look all over him, a look that promised he'd blow through Anthony like a category five hurricane if he did anything to hurt Tess.

It was a chance, and that meant another step in the right direction. They shook. "You won't regret it, sir. I'm just glad she'll be okay."

Big Tex flipped Anthony's hand over to reveal the cut knuckles and bruised fingers. "And how many attacked you again?"

"Six, Daddy," Tess said in a groggy morning voice. "They had guns."

Only one gun that Anthony knew of, but he didn't correct her. He stepped aside as Big Tex and Ray Macy went to her. Tess had called them mother hens, but they looked more like bodyguards flanking her bed. They also looked like two relieved men, both of whom loved her very much.

Quietly retreating from the room, Anthony gave them some privacy, drained by his own sense of relief, by how much he wanted to feel as though he belonged in that room.

But he didn't, not yet, no matter how much he cared about her. So he walked to the patient pantry, tossed the cold dregs of coffee into the sink then poured more. Downing it in a swallow, he threw the cup in the trash and headed to the nurses' station to consider his next step.

As far as Anthony was concerned, he and Tess were in this together, and they should solve it that way. Whether or not the reason for the attack began with letters to Big Tex, he'd almost gotten his head broken last night. That gave him some rights.

And no one would get close enough to hurt Tess again. They'd have to get through him first. *If* he could convince her to stick close…

"DiLeo." Ray Macy stepped out of the room and motioned him back. "Tess wants you."

He liked the sound of that and headed down the hall, feeling hopeful that something good might come from this brush with bad luck, after all.

He tried to get a read on Big Tex, but didn't know the man enough to guess his mood, except to recognize the air of tension was gone.

Moving to the side of the bed, Anthony inclined his head as Big Tex retreated, joining Ray Macy. Neither man left the room.

Tess watched him with a sleepy smile, and she reached up to take his hand and pull him down beside her.

Twining his fingers through hers, he held on, needing the anchor of touch. "You're one helluva driver, *chère.*"

Green fire flashed in those beautiful eyes as she examined his bruised fingers. Until that moment, Anthony hadn't fully appreciated how much he needed to see her smile to trust she'd be okay.

"Where did you learn to fight like that?"

"Did I mention my brother Damon owns a dojo and holds black belts in four disciplines?"

She gave a soft laugh. "No, you didn't. Is Damon older or younger?"

"Younger."

"So you've spent your whole life trying not to let him kick your butt?"

He smiled.

She smiled back. But her smile faded as she searched his face, and he could see how bad he must look reflected in her expression. "Why didn't you let them stitch that cut?"

"Now what makes you think I didn't *let* them?"

"Right. Did they treat you at all or did you sit here all night worrying about me?"

Funny how easily she saw through him, and since he couldn't think of any reply, he said nothing.

Tess wasn't having any part of it. "Daddy's here. Did you tell him about your service—"

"About my service center?" He forced a laugh. "Figured I'd have plenty of time to impress him with my credentials after we tracked down who was responsible for last night."

She eyed him curiously, but let the subject drop. "Daddy and Uncle Ray filled me in. My car's a mess, isn't it?"

He supposed a girl had to have priorities. Here she sat in a hospital bed with a cast on her arm after a night spent sleeping off shock, and her first thought was her car.

No, he corrected himself. Her *second* thought was her car. Her first had been about him.

Anthony found that promising, too.

"Nothing that can't be fixed, *chère*. I told the police to impound it, so she'll be safe and sound until you decide what you want to do."

"Have her towed home, I guess. I don't know of anyone around here I'd trust to do the work."

"We'll take care of it, sweet thing," Ray Macy said from the door. "Don't you worry your pretty head about her."

"Thanks, Uncle Ray." She gave an absent nod. "I'm so sorry you got caught up in all this, Anthony."

She thumbed his swollen knuckles, another absent gesture that fueled his resolve not to let her go.

"I'm not worried about *me*. But our trip's been cut short, so what about you coming back to New Orleans for a while?"

She just blinked in surprise. Anthony could practically feel the stares boring holes through the back of his head and hoped he wasn't pushing his luck *too* far.

"With everything that's just happened, the safest place for my daughter is at home," Big Tex said.

"I disagree, sir. If Tess heads back to her normal routine, she'll be predictable, and that's exactly what she doesn't want to be right now. At least not until my friends get a lock on what's going on." He turned to face the men, and found not one but *two* stares that could have drilled holes through his skull. "And to be frank, I can't convince her that she wants to keep seeing me with you two around."

Big Tex and Ray Macy scowled.

Tess laughed that silvery laugh and said, "Not to worry, Daddy. Anthony earned his chance to convince me, and I've been dying for a ride in his Firebird."

12

"I'M SURPRISED you didn't ask one of your brothers to pick us up from the airport," Tess said, resting her head on his shoulder as the taxi drove through the dark streets.

Daddy had insisted they all fly out of San Francisco on his private plane, which had dropped him and Uncle Ray off in Lubbock before continuing on to New Orleans.

Tess knew he worried about not bringing her home. He'd have much rather Anthony disembarked in Lubbock instead of taking her to New Orleans. But she'd wanted to go. Daddy's compromise had been a flight together to discuss investigation strategy and get to know Anthony.

"Don't be," he said. "If everyone knows I'm home, we'll spend the next few days bombarded with company. I promised your father I'd keep you safe and make sure you got some rest."

"So you're mother-henning me, too?"

He only rested his cheek on the top of her head, but Tess didn't doubt if she could see his face, he'd be smiling. Macho man loved this, no doubt. But even worse was that her protest came purely by rote. Having Daddy, Uncle Ray and Anthony around her all day had proven just how much she'd wanted them there.

Whoever was behind the attack had achieved his goal.

The violence had unnerved her, and Tess wondered if Anthony sensed she was still reeling. She knew her daddy did. That had been the only reason he hadn't given her a hard time about going to New Orleans with Anthony. He might not understand how she could feel safe with a man she'd only just met, but he knew she did. And he seemed willing to trust that.

That in itself felt like an accomplishment of sorts. For so long she'd dismissed his worries as invalid, considered his concerns a parental side effect of losing her mother. And while he definitely was overprotective, Tess had to admit she'd lost her perspective, too.

This was something she'd have to sort out—after they'd figured out who was behind the attack.

Snuggling closer, Tess let her eyes drift shut, trying to feel bad because she'd dragged Anthony into a situation that had turned into such a mess. She'd insisted the doctor check him out and he'd finally agreed. His ribs hadn't been cracked but bruised. Ice packs and antiseptic had taken care of the worst of the cuts and swelling, but he'd waited too long to have the gash stitched. He'd have a nice scar to remind him of the choice.

But as bad as she felt, Tess couldn't lie to herself. She was glad they were still together. The idea of an anonymous someone wanting to hurt Daddy and the people he loved, and even the people around her, was frightening, but she flat-out refused to live as an emotional hostage.

Between the San Francisco police department, Anthony's investigator friends and Daddy's chief of security at AutoCarTex, they would uncover the threat and put a stop to it. Until then, she'd enjoy her time with Anthony and let him play mother hen if that's what he wanted. He had another chance to impress her daddy, and he'd earned that chance.

She enjoyed the ride through the city, the sound of Anthony's voice as he directed the driver along a street in the Art District to his place. Though it was late, street lamps washed the facades of what appeared to be businesses that had been converted into town houses.

The taxi pulled up in front of an iron fence and ivy-covered gate. Tess waited while Anthony got out, unfolding himself as though every muscle in his body screamed with the effort. He extended a hand to her and helped her out behind him.

"You're sore, aren't you?" she asked.

"Sat too long on the plane."

While her father's plane often made speedy travel possible in a pinch, it wasn't exactly a spacious ride.

She circled the taxi to grab her own bags, knowing Anthony would do the honors if she let him. He shot her a look that convinced her he knew exactly what she was doing, paid the cabbie and grabbed his own bags. "Come on, *chère.*"

The taxi pulled away and he led her through the gate and up the steps to where a lone light shone on the portico.

Tess followed him upstairs, flipping lights on and off as he gave her the nickel tour.

She liked his place. The warehouse had been converted into a contemporary design with a ceiling shooting three stories straight up and a loft-style arrangement with a master suite on the second floor and a guest room and another that Anthony used as an office on the third.

His master suite took up the entire second floor and

much of that square footage went to an outdoor patio that turned his view into a jungle.

"Wow, you've got a green thumb," she remarked, peering through the glass doors to the wild arrangement of plants and trees that she could make out with the solar-powered lights.

"I've got a plant service."

She laughed. Dropping her garment bag beside his in front of the closet, she caught him before he moved away, ran her hand along his shoulders. "How about a massage? I've still got one good hand left. I can help loosen you up."

He turned to her, and the tenderness in his expression made her heart melt. Reaching for her broken arm, he lifted it to brush his mouth across her fingers. It was a featherlight kiss that managed to ripple through her as softly as a caress. This man had calmly soothed her panic when she'd been frantic to outrun that SUV, had fiercely protected her. She was struck by the desire to pamper him, to ease his aches and be as possessive of him as he'd been of her.

"Will you let me make you feel better?" She met his gaze above their clasped hands, and the longing in his bedroom eyes mirrored her own.

"If it involves my spa."

"My pleasure."

She unpacked their bags as he headed onto the patio to remove the protective cover and get the jets whirring to life.

After hanging clothes haphazardly in the closet and making piles on top of his dresser, Tess went on a research expedition for something to drink. She headed back downstairs, seeking out light switches to lead her way through the house that struck her as totally Anthony. Contemporary. The leather furniture seemed comfortable yet created a stylish look that suggested a designer had helped decorate the interior. Yet Anthony had imprinted himself all over the place, too.

Meticulously assembled models of classic cars on shelves above a desk. Framed photos in various disarray on practically every surface of the room. Someone had hand-crocheted a bright afghan that he'd tossed over the back of a recliner.

Sports equipment—baseball judging by the bat—had been tossed on the foyer floor, suggesting he'd walked in the door, dropped everything and hadn't given it another thought.

Tess decided this was a house he lived in, Making her way into the kitchen, she dug through his cabinets, taking stock of all the empty space, smiling when she thought about his familiarity with fast food. There was something about seeing these little things that added to the strange sense of reality she'd had ever since opening her eyes in the hospital. On the road Anthony had seemed like a fantasy man with his incredible mouth and oh-so-noble gestures.

But after last night… Tess wasn't sure exactly what it was, but last night had somehow changed everything. She'd known he had a family, brothers, a business, but seeing his home, pictures of people important to him, seeing him tired and hurt from the fight made him much more…*real*.

She opened and closed cabinets, looking for something to wrap her cast. She lucked out and found plastic garbage bags. Bypassing a bottle of burgundy in a wine rack on the counter, she went for the fridge, where she found lots of condiments and more empty shelf space. She grabbed two bottles of water.

Heading back upstairs, she found Anthony pulling towels from a linen cabinet.

"I like your house. It looks like you." She held up the bag and said, "Almost all set. I couldn't find any tape."

"Upstairs in the office." His gaze slid to the water bottles. "Didn't I have any wine?"

"You took painkillers."

"Not since we left San Francisco."

She hadn't taken any since, either, but Tess didn't have a clue how long it would take the medication to clear their systems. Slipping her arms around his waist she pressed her hips suggestively against him. "I won't take chances. I want to make love to you, not send you back to the hospital."

"Making love definitely sounds better."

"If you can move, of course."

"I can always move enough for that, *chère*." To prove his point, he ground a promising erection against her. She tipped her face up to his for a kiss, enjoying this unfamiliar tenderness, wanting to explore it.

She meant just to give him a gentle peck, but his mouth covered hers slowly, heavily almost, and she could taste his weariness. She held him even tighter. He sighed.

The sound broke against her mouth, and she drank it in, savoring his warm breath, the unfamiliar feel of his swollen lips. She pulled away then, gliding her hands around his waist to work his shirt from his jeans. With her one bum hand, and his bruised ribs, it took both of them to get the shirt over his head, and when they did, she tossed it onto the bed.

Leaning forward, she pressed her mouth softly against the bruised skin on his ribs, felt him tremble.

"Does that feel a little better?" she asked, unfastening his jeans and freeing the sexy body part that she was so enjoying becoming acquainted with.

"Do I look like I need to be taken care of?"

She wouldn't want to crush Mr. Macho Man's pride so she simply said, "I owe you."

"For what? We're only together because you gave me a chance to impress you, remember?"

"You impressed me above and beyond last night."

He exhaled sharply when he leaned over to help her lame attempts to get the pants down his legs one-handed. "I don't think I impressed you enough."

She peered up in time to catch him looking at her cast.

"Trust me when I say I can't think of another man I'd have wanted to be with last night, Anthony. I mean that."

"Your father and uncle wouldn't let anything happen to you."

"They'd have been two against six, and trust me, neither of them fight like you do. Can you imagine last night with Daryl? He'd have opened that mouth of his and wound up getting us both shot. Guaranteed."

That earned a chuckle. "Okay. You got me there."

He actually swayed on his feet and braced himself when she tugged off the last of his pants. She tossed those onto the bed, too.

"You said the office is upstairs."

He glanced absently at the door. "Yeah, I'll go grab—"

"*You* get in the tub. I can find the tape."

She headed out of the room without giving him a chance

to argue. The man was dead on his feet, and she needed to get in the spa with him before he fell asleep and drowned.

The stairway continued at the second-floor loft, and the top floor had another landing with two doors. Inside the office, a massive desk housed a late model computer setup and a variety of office equipment. Like the rest of his house, this room was stylishly decorated, but judging by the piles of paper scattered over every surface, Tess guessed that he spent a lot of time in here.

Sitting in his cushy leather chair, she scanned the desk, debating where she would hide if she were a roll of tape. Her gaze fell on a photograph displayed on a shelf beside the monitor, a spot where he might slide his gaze often while he worked.

Carefully retrieving the photo from the shelf, Tess glanced into the face of a beautiful redheaded woman who'd been captured in a candid moment, laughing, her blue eyes sparkling with humor. Tess could only see her from the neck up, but didn't need to see more to know this woman would be delicate and exquisitely feminine. It was all over her fine-boned features, the graceful way she tipped her head when she laughed.

He'd mentioned a sister, but she didn't look a thing like the man Tess had left climbing into the spa downstairs.

"Who are you?" she whispered into the quiet while replacing the frame on the shelf.

Silence was her only reply.

A roll of mailing tape hid in the desk drawer, so she grabbed it and a pair of scissors before returning to the patio where Anthony sat submerged in the spa. He cracked an eye open when she came in.

"Find what you needed?"

"Yep." Quickly removing her clothes, she deposited them beside Anthony's then tried to fashion a protective plastic covering for her cast.

"Come here, *chère*," he said, and she went to sit on the rim of the spa. "Let me do this. I'm the mechanic, remember?"

"I could never forget how good you are with your hands."

He smiled at that, his ego swelling visibly. Fashioning a watertight wrapping to her elbow, he secured it with tape.

"Feel good?" he asked.

"Perfect." She slid into the water, pleased when he pulled her onto the seat beside him.

Dangling her cast on the outer rim, she let her legs twine with his, skin meeting skin as she stretched out against him in the hot bubbly water.

He sighed, leaned his head back and closed his eyes. "Oh, man. I needed this. You feel so good."

Tess only rested her head against his shoulder, careful not to press hard against his ribs. They faded into companionable silence, letting the hot water soak away the stiffness.

Solar lights lit the patio, casting the lush summer night in a bluish glow, and the peaceful sounds even helped chase away the memories of violence.

She must have dozed because suddenly he caught her cast and directed her arm back toward the ledge. She felt dreamy and relaxed and…*content* in a way she couldn't ever remember feeling before. With him she didn't feel restless or bored, and she wanted to understand why, *needed* to understand.

Idly stroking her fingers across his tight tummy, she asked, "That picture on your desk. Who is she?"

"A friend."

"A *friend* friend or a *date* friend?"

He didn't answer right away, just stared into the night, but the jaw he clenched tight hinted at what she'd already guessed—whoever the woman was, she was important.

"A friend friend who became a date friend who's a friend friend again."

Okay. Tess waited, hoping he'd offer something more about a woman who'd apparently been in his life awhile. But they faded into silence again.

She debated cooling her curiosity, accepting what he offered and not pushing for more. He didn't have to explain himself to her. They'd signed on for a fling, and that didn't entitle her to answers.

"Tell me about her, Anthony." Her curiosity wouldn't cool. She was getting more than she bargained for with this man, and wanted to understand what was happening between them.

"She believed in me so much that I believed, too."

It wasn't at all what Tess had expected, but that simple statement held so much power, confirmed the impact this woman had had on Anthony's life.

He was silent so long that Tess thought that's all she'd get, but then he said, "Watching her conquer the world showed me I could do anything I wanted to do, be anything I wanted to be. All I had to do was believe in myself."

Tess had recognized that confidence in him from the first, began to understand. "Were you together long?"

"On and off for ten years."

Whoa. The "on and off" part raised a few questions. She

couldn't imagine what would keep bringing two people back together for that long, but she had no frame of reference. She'd never dated anyone for more than a few months, had always found some reason to move on.

That raised another important question, but not one Anthony could answer. One she'd have to tackle herself. "When did ten years end?"

"A long time ago." He stared off into the night. "Nearly five years."

For some reason Tess felt much better. "Do you mind if I ask why?"

"She didn't settle. She still doesn't."

More simple words, but the emotion in his face convinced Tess that he meant this woman hadn't settled for what he'd had to offer, hadn't settled for *him.*

She was surprised by how many emotions that thought stirred up. Sorrow for what was clearly a painful memory. Disbelief that any woman would toss this man's love away. And envy that the redhead in the picture had the power to hurt him so much.

Tess stopped asking questions then. Each one she asked left her wanting to know why she'd never cared so much for a man. Her heart felt heavy with more than hurt for his pain. For unfulfilled promises. For lives that felt empty.

And she wasn't sure whether she meant his or her own.

But now…with Anthony, she understood what it felt like to want and liked how it felt to be wanted back. A feeling of such promise that she tipped her mouth to his throat, pressed a kiss to the pulse beating there.

Snuggling against him, she let the bubbling quiet and their nearness soothe away everything but the pleasure of being together. And when he finally asked, "You ready to get out?" she smiled, excited at the thought of climbing into his bed.

Getting out of the spa, she grabbed a towel, dragging the soft cotton over her skin, sensing Anthony's gaze on her. She put on a show, liking the way he made her feel, more than beautiful, as if she was the most important thing in his world.

He helped her remove the plastic from her cast, then it was her turn to watch when he stood in an eye-catching if drowsy display of dripping male. Tess brushed aside his hands. "Let me."

He half sat on the rim of the spa while she ruffled the towel along his shoulders, down his arms, gingerly patting his ribs, the broken skin on his hands. She explored him with an unfamiliar sense of possession, of power, to ease his pain, to bring him pleasure.

He groaned softly when she worked the towel over his groin, lingering passes along wet skin that earned an immediate reaction. So she sank to her knees to press whisper-soft kisses in the wake of her touch. He groaned again, threaded his fingers into her hair and hung on.

Tess laughed and nuzzled her face against his groin again, nipped her way along that tender spot at the juncture of his thigh, dragged her tongue along puckered skin.

"Is this payback for the broken arm?" he asked.

"Yes." And to prove it, she licked the underside of his penis, gratified when his growing erection jumped toward her mouth like a pleasure-seeking missile. "Now let's go to bed, so I can pay you back some more."

She didn't have to tell him twice, and when they slid beneath the sheets, they became a tangle of glowing skin and drowsy eagerness. With a burst of energy that came from nowhere, he rolled and braced himself on top of her, staring down with a satisfied smile.

"What?" she asked.

"I wanted to see how you look in my bed."

"Tired, I'll bet."

"No, *chère,* you look good…good enough to eat."

She laughed, wishing he could have obliged her but with those swollen lips…Tess slithered her legs around him instead, aligned herself….

"What are you doing?"

Her fingers around his erection answered that question. He swelled in her hand, his body recognizing what she had in mind. Dragging him against her moist heat, she took aim, and fired. He arched his hips to go the rest of the way.

Tess sighed.

Anthony sighed.

And they lay in the darkness, swaying gently against each other. Their motions dreamy and lazy and sweet. Their bodies fitted perfectly as the night closed in around them.

Tess stared into his face, resisting the urge to kiss his mouth, watching her pleasure mirrored in his expression.

Their breaths broke in soft bursts as they rose toward fulfillment, the feeling so amazing and complete that she knew all these tender emotions—the curiosity, the hurt, the ecstasy—could come with only this man. Only Anthony.

Swaying full-bodied against him, she dug her fingers into his butt when he rallied the energy to drive harder, riding all those places that made her ache, only to withdraw in sleek strokes, an ebb and flow that wound her toward fulfillment. Then she exploded with him, lazy, crazy bursts that went on and on.

Only Anthony.

13

TESS DIDN'T LEAVE Anthony's place for another two days. Anthony had insisted—and she'd agreed—that since they'd been cheated of their minivacation from the real world, they deserved to indulge their convalescence.

When food had become an issue, they'd ordered pizza delivery, and for two glorious days and three glorious nights, they'd done nothing more than make love, soak in the spa, sleep, munch on reheated pizza and work their way through a bottle of ibuprofen.

Tess enjoyed this break from reality and, aside from telephone calls to Daddy, the time passed in a blur of dreamy pleasure and incredible orgasms, where she spoiled Anthony and let Anthony spoil her. And in between she tried to make sense of how she felt about him.

Eventually reality intruded.

"Good morning, *chère*," Anthony whispered close to her ear, a burst of tingly warmth that seemed the perfect way to start a new day. "I ate the last slice of pizza before bed last night, so I'm heading out for breakfast. Any requests?"

"Protein."

He trailed kisses over her temples, down her cheek. "Sleep. I won't be long. I'll lock you in with the security system and wake you when I get back."

Those feather kisses made her want to drag him back down into bed, but to do that, she'd have had to move. No go. After spending so many days depleting as much strength as they'd regained, Tess found it all too tempting to roll over and go to sleep. She was pretty sure he'd almost killed her with his particular brand of mouth therapy sometime during the night.

Or had that been the night before last?

Death by orgasm. No doubt Penny would say, "Way to go!"

Tess must have slept again because the next thing she heard was a male voice. She didn't bother opening her eyes, only vaguely aware of the rich masculine sound and a hunger that seemed out of proportion with how awake she wasn't. She wondered dreamily what Anthony had managed for breakfast, heard a steady stream of talk that grew louder as footsteps thumped up the stairs.

He said he'd awaken her, but if he expected her to open her eyes without sprinkling her face with more of those tempting kisses, the man had another think coming.

Then came a knock.

Her eyes opened, and Tess stared at the door. Were Anthony's hands so full he couldn't get the door? She tried to rally the energy to get up, but as sleep cleared her brain, she realized the voice on the other side of the door only *sounded* like Anthony.

She shot from zero to sixty in a blink.

Bolting upright, she clutched the sheet to her chest, undecided between hunkering down or bolting for the bathroom. Another knock. More chatter. The image of being caught bare-assed as she raced across the room froze her to the spot.

Then the door opened.

"Is there really a woman in here?" a male voice asked, a voice familiar, yet strikingly unfamiliar.

Tess had a moment of panic as she watched the door open wider, but decided to whack anyone who got close enough with her cast. A head appeared, followed by broad shoulders, and a face that was Anthony, but wasn't. Younger and leaner, this DiLeo brother—and there could be no doubt he was one of Anthony's brothers—wore his hair *really* long and grinned a faster grin.

"Well, hello, green eyes," he said. "We didn't believe Anthony when he said he had a woman up here. But you're a woman all right, and a gorgeous one."

We?

Before Tess had a chance to reflect on who else might be here—please, God, not his mother!—or to wonder why no one believed Anthony had invited a woman home, another tawny head popped through the door.

This brother—and there could be no missing that here was yet another of Anthony's brothers—shouldered the door even wider to give her a glimpse of an older and brawnier version of these cookie-cutter DiLeo siblings.

This one wore his hair short and wasn't nearly so quick to grin. In fact, as he raked his gaze over her, he seemed to be summing her up before saying, "He was telling the truth."

"Do you believe it?"

The older DiLeo only shook his head, and they both turned back to stare at her as if they'd never seen a woman in their combined lifetimes.

She glanced at the bedside clock, tried not to think about the impression she must be making, so clearly naked in the middle of their brother's rumpled bed.

"Good morning, gentlemen." She wouldn't win this race if she didn't get behind the wheel. "The name's Tess. Anthony stepped out. He said he wouldn't be long."

They exchanged glances as if they'd never heard a woman talk before today, either.

"Tess from Texas." the younger brother said.

The older brother leveled his gaze her way again, and she was relieved when he didn't budge from the doorway to do something gentlemanly like shake her hand. "Dominic DiLeo. Anthony's oldest brother. This is Damon, the family pain in the ass. I tried to catch him before he got upstairs. My apologies."

"Like you could catch me, Nic." Damon laughed. "Actually, I'm the brother who's not happy that Anthony caught the prettiest gal between here and Houston."

"Lubbock," she corrected.

He inclined his head. "We heard Anthony got back to town. When he didn't call, we decided to find out why."

"When did he get back?" Nic asked.

"Thursday night."

"Did you come back with him, green eyes?"

She nodded.

"He told us he had company, but we didn't believe him." Nic gave her the first thing that resembled a smile.

"You saw him? He's on his way home?"

"Not anytime soon."

Damon's grin almost made her afraid to ask why. "Why?"

"He's downstairs. Handcuffed to Nic's cruiser."

"Handcuffed?"

Nic nodded. "I'm surprised you didn't hear him. He didn't go down without a fight. Never does."

Another fight?

She wasn't sure whether or not to take them seriously and wanted a peek outside for herself. However, these two didn't look as if they'd be voluntarily leaving this room in the immediate future. They were checking her out, and she got the sense they were also taking her measure.

Concern for Anthony finally won out, so hanging on to the sheet for dear life, she swung her legs around and stood, whipping yards of high-thread-count sateen around her. Then as regally as if she'd crossed the finish line a car length ahead of the pack, she made for the window.

Sure enough, there was a NOPD cruiser with visibars flashing. Anthony leaned against it, still holding a bag— presumably their breakfast. He bristled with attitude, and she bit back a smile when he saw her. Pushing away from the car, he motioned to a hand still firmly attached to the door handle.

Clutching the sheet in place with her cast, she wrestled the window open with the other. "Are you okay?"

"Tell them they're dead."

No need to ask who "them" was.

"Tell him that busted-up face of his has me real worried," Damon shot back.

Nic's stoic gaze zeroed in on her wrist. "Does that cast have anything to do with what happened to Anthony's face?"

She nodded.

Damon swore. "I told him to get his ass into the dojo more than twice a week. He might have done a better job protecting you, green eyes."

Tess had no idea if Anthony had even called his family while they were on the road. If he had, he obviously hadn't said anything about the attack. She didn't want to interfere with how he handled them, but she wasn't going to stand here and listen to his brother abuse him, either.

"If you're the brother with black belts in four disciplines, then you should know he held his own just fine. Six men with guns attacked us in San Francisco. Anthony had nothing more than a tire iron and me with my pepper spray."

"You're…*defending* him?"

She wasn't going to dignify *that* with a reply, especially when Nic's frown had deepened into a scowl. "So what happened to the six men with the guns?"

"Three out cold. One ran screaming. He questioned the others."

"This wasn't a random attack?" Nic asked.

"No, but if you want more information, you'll have to talk to him." She glanced back through the window. "And just out of curiosity, when do you plan to let him go?"

"As soon as you're ready to leave."

"Where am I going?"

"It's Sunday," Damon said as if that explained everything.

Nic glanced at his watch. "Mama will have dinner on the table in about thirty minutes. Better get a move on."

Tess wanted to make a good impression with Anthony's family—better than this first meeting anyway—but her clothing choices were limited since they hadn't gotten out of bed long enough to wash a load of clothes. Even a quick shower was out of the question. The hassle of wrapping her cast aside, Tess wouldn't leave Anthony handcuffed on the street any longer than necessary. Although she wouldn't have minded making these two wait one bit.

So she settled for heading into the bathroom to perform damage control, and reemerged an impressive ten minutes later, fully dressed with minty-fresh breath and neatly made-up face and hair that wouldn't frighten kids or dogs.

Nic had moved to stand beside the window, but Damon still stood beside the door, eyeing her with a wicked look.

"The loveliest lady in Lubbock, I'd say."

"Ready, Tess?" Nic glanced down at the street again, looking as though he wanted to get this show on the road.

Served him right as far as Tess was concerned. "In a sec. I want to grab a few things for Anthony. He didn't shower yet."

Nic and Damon exchanged glances again, but Tess didn't understand what *they* didn't understand. They'd attacked the man on the street before he'd even had breakfast.

Nic nodded to Damon, who dutifully went to the closet. Tess grabbed Anthony's duffel bag—still half-packed since they hadn't gotten around to unpacking yet, either— and dumped everything except his toiletries on the bed.

"No, not that one," she told Damon, who was pulling a polo-style shirt off a hanger. "Something that buttons."

"Why?"

"He bruised his ribs. It's hard for him to lift his arms."

"Oh, the poor baby." Damon slipped the shirt back into the closet and got another. "Is that what you've been doing here, green eyes—nursing my big bro back to health?"

Tess realized that Damon wasn't only the family pain in the ass, but very protective of his big brother. She liked what that said about him, and found her mood softening a little. A very little. At least until they uncuffed Anthony.

"If you must know, we've been nursing *each other* back to health. Doctor's orders."

That won a laugh from Nic, which Tess guessed was a rare occurrence. "Here's hoping he feels a lot better when he sees you, Tess. Otherwise he'll have to jog alongside my cruiser because I'm not unlocking those handcuffs."

To her relief, Anthony's mood did seem to improve the minute he laid eyes on her. Those big brown eyes melted over her in an apology he didn't need to make.

"You okay?" she asked.

"I *almost* made it with breakfast," he said wryly, narrowing his gaze at his brothers, who were still standing on the stairs.

"I hear your mom will have dinner on the table soon."

He tossed the bag onto the back dash. "Whatever she's cooking will beat this shrimp étouffé from Toujacques."

"Shrimp étouffé for breakfast?"

"You said you wanted protein, *chère*."

She smiled gratefully then motioned to Nic. "He seems in fine spirits. Let him go."

"What, you don't have the energy to jog home, big bro?" Damon smiled, but not Anthony, and she didn't miss how Nic gave his younger brother a head start to lock himself inside the front seat before he released Anthony.

They climbed into the back, and Tess scooted close enough to whisper, "First an ambulance. Now a police cruiser. Being with you is a thrill a minute."

"Told you we'd have a good time together." Anthony pounded on the Plexiglas divider separating the front seat. "How the hell did you two find out I was home?"

Damon slid open a panel. "The Gooch saw you at the casino. He called the house to find out if Mama had cancelled dinner since you were raiding the VIP bar."

"The Gooch?" Tess asked.

"A friend," Anthony said. "I'm not sure whose, though. He just showed up one day and never left. But leave it to him to still be gambling this late on a Sunday."

"What, you expected him to be in church?" Damon asked, and something about that made all three brothers laugh.

Tess remembered what Courtney Gerard had said about being adopted by the DiLeo family, and felt an unfamiliar zip of…*something* at the thought of meeting Anthony's family—extended or otherwise—a crazy mix of nerves and excitement.

Anthony's family home was a modest two story in a residential neighborhood skirting the French Quarter. The yard was meticulously cared for with a colorful array of blooms dripping over the fence. Cars crammed the driveway and overflowed onto the street, and while the place looked barely large enough to raise a family with six kids, it had a friendly feel that said, "Welcome."

"You grew up here?" she asked Anthony as Nic maneuvered the cruiser into a tight space on the street.

He nodded, and she liked this glimpse into his life, another piece of the puzzle that was Anthony of the noble gestures and the wicked mouth. She could see him and his brothers running wild around this place with their friends growing up, wondered at the woman who ruled this roost single-handedly and raised such a nice son.

She might even be warming up to Nic and Damon. Even though they'd handcuffed Anthony to the car and left him standing in the street, they were all clearly fond of each other with an easy camaraderie that was fun to watch.

"Let me go warn Mama that you've brought a girl home. I don't want her to have a heart attack." Damon hopped out of the cruiser and shot off down the stone walkway.

"Damned big mouth." Anthony snorted in disgust as he hauled his duffel bag over his shoulder and extended a hand to Tess.

"You should have called," Nic chided.

"I would have when I wanted to see your ugly mug."

They reached the front door just as Damon burst down a hallway, yelling, "Anthony got back into town on *Thursday*."

His hand tightened around hers possessively as he led her into a huge kitchen filled with people. Tess didn't even get to look around before a woman with a hint of Italian in her voice demanded, "*Caro mio,* you made it home, but didn't call?"

Anthony didn't get a chance to reply before Damon drew up against the woman with the tawny blond hair, standing in front of the stove. He kissed her cheek. "Anthony *and Tess* have been nursing each other back to health, Mama. Doctor's orders."

"Tess?" Mrs. DiLeo turned around to have a look for herself. "What doctor?"

She was a small woman, who hardly looked big enough, or old enough for that matter, to have reared these DiLeo boys. Her gaze zeroed in on her son's face and her expression dissolved into a frown. "Anthony, you been fighting? And who's your girl?"

With another of those reassuring smiles, Anthony looped his arm through Tess's and led her in state across the kitchen.

Mrs. DiLeo might have been physically petite, but there was nothing small about her presence. Meticulously groomed, from stylishly short hair to designer sandals, she was a beautiful woman with smooth olive skin and dark snapping eyes. This kitchen was obviously her throne room.

"Mama, this is Tess Hardaway. Tess, my mother, Angelina."

"It's a pleasure, Mrs. DiLeo." She extended her hand.

Anthony's mom shook with a no-nonsense grip, and didn't let go. She drew Tess toward her for a closer look. "You're a beauty. You've been taking good care of my Anthony?"

"I've been trying, ma'am. He's giving me a run for my money."

A smile twitched around Mrs. DiLeo's mouth as her hand slid from Tess's. She reached up to gingerly touch the healing wound on Anthony's face. "You think that looks dashing, don't you?"

"Is that why you wouldn't let the doctor stitch you up?" Tess asked.

Anthony flashed a smile that made her feel all flushed and fluttery and aware that not only his mom, but also everyone in the room hung on to their every word. "It worked, didn't it? You're here, *chère*."

"Of course I'm here." Tess rolled her eyes. "You begged me to come, didn't you?"

There was a beat of silence before snickers erupted around the kitchen, and even Tess couldn't suppress a smile when his mom nodded approvingly.

"Call me Mama, Tess," she said. "Everyone does. Now grab a seat and let's eat."

Two places at the table miraculously appeared, and suddenly she and Anthony plunged into the thick of things.

Tempting dishes appeared. Wine flowed. Conversation happened and laughter rang out. Tess was reminded of feeding time at the Critchley ranch, always a chaotic affair whenever she had the good fortune to show up in Mrs. Critchley's big kitchen at feeding time.

Tess met Marc, the brother in between Anthony and Nic, a man with a rolling laugh and a penchant for adventure as he blew in and out of town with his work as a bounty hunter.

She met Vince, the youngest, whom everyone called Vinny despite his repeated corrections. He'd just come off his shift at Charity Hospital, where he was doing his residency, and still looked sleep ruffled around the edges from a nap on the living-room sofa.

No sight of the one and only DiLeo daughter, but Tess did meet the Gooch, a startlingly attractive man who was close to Nic's age. He might radiate testosterone like the rest of this crew, but his wavy black hair and icy green eyes set him miles apart. And that glinting gold earring…he looked like a rogue.

She remembered what Anthony had said about not knowing when he'd first showed up or to whom he belonged. But the Gooch clearly belonged. She had no clue what his real name might be, but he sat at this huge table telling stories, as much a part of this family as any of the brothers.

There was a nail tech from Mama DiLeo's hair salon and two of Anthony's mechanics, who'd contributed freshly baked Italian bread and cannolis from the only bakery in town, consensus was, that could make a decent cannoli.

There was a lot of good-natured ribbing—especially when someone brought up the subject of work.

"You own a dojo, Damon," Marc said in a tone dripping disdain. "When the hell are you going to get a real job?"

"When you stay home long enough to take your turn on Mama detail," Damon shot back.

"What's Mama detail?" Tess asked.

"Mama doesn't drive, so we all take turns as chauffeur," Anthony explained. "Except for Marc, who's conveniently never here when his week rolls around."

"What did I tell you?" Damon shot a scowling Marc a smug look. "Like I make this stuff up."

Nic shook his head as if they all were crazy. "I can't figure this. Would be easier for Mama if she just took the driving test. Then she wouldn't have to put up with any of you."

"Makes perfect sense to me," Tess said. "What mother would want to miss out on having her boys drive her around? Especially when it seems to make you all feel so important."

Mama DiLeo raised her wineglass in salute.

Marc hooted with laughter. "I think I'm going to like you, Tess. You won't take any of Anthony's shit."

She sank back in her chair and whispered for Anthony's ears alone, "What shit?"

"No shit, *chère*," he said in that whiskey voice. "What you see is what you get with me. My brother's an idiot."

She sipped her wine to contain a smile as Marc eyed them as if he suspected he was the topic of their discussion.

Then the family moved on to another topic for debate, giving her enough time to eat before they demanded the details of her meeting with Anthony.

Tess wasn't in public relations without good reason, and when the spotlight shone her way, she ran with it.

"Y'all know the Nostalgic Car Club hosted their annual convention in town last week, right?"

Several nods, and Nic narrowed his gaze. "Ran a bunch of fools through lockup because they couldn't keep their speedometers under a hundred while driving through my town."

"No one should have been doing a hundred except at Dixie Downs, Nic. That's the only time I drove a hundred. You have my word." She held up her hand in a gesture of honor.

Anthony laughed, but Damon sank back in his chair and eyed her curiously. "What were you doing on the track, green eyes?"

"Lapping the best of them. At least until I looked in my rearview mirror and saw this man's Firebird in my draft."

That raised a few eyebrows and Tess knew she was on a roll. She reveled in it, describing the scene with animated hand motions. "So I start blipping him, you know, just playing a little to see what he's made of, and, wham, the second I slide coming out of a turn, he shoots around me and I'm riding his bumper all the way to the finish line."

As Tess's words faded, all eyes turned to Anthony. He opened his mouth to comment then jerked forward in his chair when Marc slapped the back of his head.

"Didn't we teach you anything?" Marc said. "You don't beat a lady on the track. You're lucky she's even talking to you."

"Jeez. It wasn't my fault." Anthony rubbed the back of his head. "She provoked me."

"Ah, what did you do to provoke him, Tess?" the Gooch asked in a Cajun drawl that made her think of pirates in the bayou.

"It wasn't me, it was my car. He thinks it's ugly."

"I *never* called your car ugly."

"What do you drive?" Vince asked.

"A purple Gremlin," Anthony said, and there wasn't a man at that table who didn't wince.

It was enough to hurt a girl's feelings. "Let me tell you about my purple Gremlin, gentlemen. She gave this man and his muscle car a run for his money."

"*You* gave *Anthony* a run for his money on the track?" the mechanic named Sal asked incredulously.

"Not her car, trust me." Anthony sounded more than a little defensive. "But Tess isn't any normal driver, either. Tell them who taught you to race, *chère.*"

"My uncle."

Anthony snorted. "Her uncle, the *Maverick.*"

More silence, then all at once…

"*You're Ray Macy's niece?*"

"*Number seven? We call him the exterminator.*"

"*He kicked some royal ass the last time he came to town.*"

Tess grinned. "Didn't help me this time around. I lost."

"Idiot." Marc took another swipe at Anthony that he neatly dodged.

"Couldn't be that big an idiot," Mama DiLeo said matter-of-factly. "Tess is sitting at my table for Sunday dinner."

"Anthony more than made up for his poor manners on the track."

"What'd he do—jog a lap naked?" Damon asked.

A retort sprang to her lips, but Tess bit it back, not sure his mom would appreciate knowing how attractive she found her son in the buff. "He started by making a very generous contribution to my favorite charity."

Nic frowned. "My cheap brother? I don't believe it. This one squeezes pennies until they cry."

"I think our Anthony was trying to impress his young lady." Mama DiLeo glanced between them.

Tess just smiled and scooped up the last bite of her eggplant Parmesan, trying to act casual beneath Mama DiLeo's knowing gaze. Anthony laughed, and no sooner had she rested the fork back on her plate than he stood and took her plate.

He returned shortly with more of the exquisite eggplant and set the plate in front of her. "Was I right, or was I right?"

There was no missing the man's pride in his mother's cooking, and she said, "You win. This sauce has ruined me for any other."

"You'll just have to make sure you're around a lot on Sundays, *chère.*"

The innuendo in that statement and the invitation in his eyes made her feel all fluttery again, but it wasn't until after Anthony reached for the breadbasket that Tess realized everyone else had fallen silent.

"Excuse me," Marc said. "Did my brother just get off his ass in the middle of dinner to serve this woman?"

"Good thing there's a doctor in the house," Vince said. "He's going to give someone a heart attack if he keeps this up."

"Behave, you two," Mama DiLeo admonished. "Anthony's impressing his young lady, and I won't have you all scaring her off." She winked at Tess then rose from the table, collected her dish and headed for the sink. "I raised a gentleman. Anthony, at least, knows how to take care of a lady."

Tess definitely wouldn't argue that. She felt comfortable sitting beside him with his family and friends, liked seeing him interact with the people he cared about, liked that the people he cared about accepted her with no questions asked. To Tess, that said a lot about how much they loved and respected him.

Talk inevitably got to the attack. Nic wanted details, so she and Anthony relayed the events of that night, and how the San Francisco police were investigating the attack locally despite Anthony's belief that the threat had followed Tess into town.

"I called Harley and asked her and Mac to investigate," Anthony said. "Haven't heard anything yet, but she said they'd drop everything to start following the trail before it got cold. I expect to hear from her soon."

"I'll give her a call and see if she needs my help cutting through any jurisdictional bullshit with the San Francisco police. That might save some time."

"Thanks, Nic," Anthony said.

"Am I hearing this right?" Damon let his fork clatter to his plate, the devil all over him. "You called Red from San Francisco, but we had to drag you out of bed after you'd been home for three days?"

Tess took her cue to get up from the table and remove their plates to the sink. Damon was a troublemaker, and she simply couldn't face a public discussion about how he and Nic had caught her in bed this morning. Not in front of an audience that included their mom, even if she seemed to be enjoying the show.

"I needed Harley on the trail," Anthony said. "If I'd called, half of New Orleans would have shown up at my place."

Tess heard a few snorts of laughter and one disbelieving, "Yeah, right."

"I already told you we needed rest. Doctor's orders, remember?" she asked, feigning innocence. "Anthony shouldn't be left handcuffed to a car on the street in his condition."

"Dominic Joseph and Damon Francis, you *handcuffed* your brother to the car?"

Suddenly they were in the hot seat, each attempting to blame the other for the idea. Unfortunately, Mama DiLeo didn't seem too interested in their explanations, and Tess felt a momentary pang of regret when she remembered Anthony's story about the knife. Then again, better Nic's and Damon's butts, than a conversation about her in Anthony's bed. Merciless, true, but it looked like every man for himself with the DiLeos.

Or every woman. And Tess wanted to get off to a good start.

"Nicely done." Anthony joined her at the counter as she was buying time by pouring coffee.

She pressed a mug into his hands. "As long as Mama doesn't start hurling silverware."

"She always misses. Intentionally. Got a helluvan arm, that woman does."

Tess remembered the baseball gear in his foyer and wondered if he'd inherited that arm, but before she got a chance to ask, Mama showed up.

"*Caro mio,* I took care of your brothers, but you didn't say how your work went? Did Tess's father see your proposal?"

Tess listened curiously, surprised when Anthony didn't answer but exploded away from the counter, swearing and sloshing coffee over the rim of his mug.

"Goddamn it, Mama." He set the mug down, making even more of a mess. Swinging around, he glared accusingly at his mom, who only smiled, raised a pair of shears and...*his ponytail.*

Tess stared as everyone dissolved into laughter.

Anthony rubbed the back of his nape, scowling. "Now you've got to give me a haircut."

"Come to the shop tomorrow." Mama waved him off and headed to the trash to deposit the tawny locks. "You know I hate cutting hair in the kitchen. I like my chair and mirror—"

"Come on, Tess," he said. "We'll have to skip dessert. If we hurry, I can catch Lou at the barbershop."

Mama scowled. Anthony scowled back.

A power struggle waged, and everyone in the kitchen had a ringside seat.

Anthony tossed his hands up in exasperation. "Here I finally bring a girl home, and now we have to leave—"

"Oh, all right." Mama tossed up her hands, too, and started issuing orders. "Vinny, get my salon bag. Tess, Gooch, Sal, let's get this food off the table before it winds up covered in hair."

Everyone leaped into action, and Anthony winked as he grabbed a chair and spun it into the center of the kitchen.

"You're it, Marc," he said. "Think you'll be around long enough to take your turn this time?"

"Damn things I do for this family," Marc grumbled in reply, running a hand through his hair.

Damon laughed as he sidled up against her at the sink, where she began scraping plates for the dishwasher.

"Marc's turn for what?" she asked.

"Mama's a hairdresser, green eyes." He lifted his long

ponytail. "She's been after *this* since I grew it, so the rest of them take turns growing their own puny ones to distract her. Even the Gooch."

"And now it's Marc's turn?"

Damon nodded. "It's become a family game."

But it was more than a game in Tess's eyes. Anthony's long hair wasn't a sign of rebelliousness, but an act that showed how much he cared for his brother. And as she loaded the dishwasher, she thought about brothers who took turns chauffeuring their mother around, who grew out ponytails for surprise haircuts and involved themselves in each others' lives.

While it might be every man for himself with the Di-Leos, this family clearly stuck together when it counted.

Tess liked what that said about them.

She liked it a lot.

Vince returned with Mama's salon bag and a package of multicolored permanent markers that he plunked down on the counter beside her. "While Anthony gets his hair cut, we'll sign your cast. The thing's so white it's blinding me."

Leave it to a doctor to notice. Tess was too busy noticing how Anthony's haircut shaped up. The close sides seemed to emphasize the sculpted lines of his face and make him even more striking. He looked different, but she liked the difference.

"I can't believe Anthony didn't do the honors." Damon agreed, snatching a blue marker. "He knows cast etiquette better than the rest of us."

Marc showed up and snatched the marker out of his hand. "Not better than you. Didn't you beat him when you broke your hand trying to karate chop cinder blocks or something?"

Damon frowned. "I don't think so. Mama, who broke the most bones?"

Just looking at this crew, Tess had no trouble imagining frequent visits to the emergency room.

"Frankie," Mama said. "She beat Damon with her broken ankle."

"I remember that." Marc gingerly directed Tess's arm to the counter for support then went to work on her cast like an artist. "She pulled the whole damn drainpipe off the side of the house trying to sneak out at night."

She. Frankie must be the one and only DiLeo sister.

"And she walked around with that broken ankle for a week so Mama wouldn't know," Vince said.

My brother doesn't deserve you. Marc wrote the word *doesn't* in bright orange for emphasis.

He beamed at his handiwork, and Tess wondered what she'd gotten herself into here. Not only would this cast be a permanent part of her wardrobe for a few weeks, but everyone seemed to assume that she was on her way to becoming a permanent fixture in Anthony's life.

But she only smiled as Damon wrote in green marker. *Green Eyes, you're the loveliest lady in Lubbock.*

Nic wrote a more conventional: *Hope you get this cast off soon!* Vince wrote underneath it: *It's getting uglier by the second!* with a big yellow smiley face.

Even the Gooch joined in with a *Welcome to the family.*

Vince grabbed the red marker before Sal could. "Let's save this one for Anthony so he can draw little red hearts."

Tess glanced at Anthony with his wet hair and styling cape covering all that yummy terrain between his neck and knees. He narrowed his gaze at his youngest brother then looked at her…and the pleasure softening his handsome face made her want to hand him the red marker herself.

14

"THIS BIG DAY YOU HAD TO get back for is a trip to school?" Tess stared out the Firebird's window as Anthony wheeled into a parking lot, clearly in the throes of first-day madness.

"Not a trip to any school. Today is my goddaughter's first day at preschool."

"Oh, well, that is big news."

"Yep. Sure is."

He made a parking spot on the grass at the back of the lot beneath a sign that read No Parking. Tess just rolled her eyes and followed him inside, mulling over his casual disregard for parking laws and his devotion to the people he cared about.

She liked how much importance he placed on a little girl's big day and that he wanted to share that day with her.

It was another piece in the puzzle that was Anthony.

He led her inside an old but well-maintained building, and they battled their way down a crowded hall.

Tess had no idea who they were looking for, but she knew when they found his goddaughter because a child's voice rang out. "Uncle Anthony!"

Anthony sank to his knees just as a small redheaded missile launched herself into his arms.

He hugged the child tight, pressing a kiss to the top of her head. "Hey, little princess. All set for your big day?"

"Mommy gave me braids." Stepping out of his arms, the little princess shook her head from side to side to display two long braids that looked as if Mommy had to wrestle a lot of hair to make them. Fine red curls were already creeping out, and all the shaking dislodged a few more.

"I like 'em. But then you're always gorgeous."

"I know," she said matter-of-factly, earning a smile from her doting uncle. Then her clear gray gaze riveted to the plastic box he held. "Is that for me?"

"I'd never show up on your big day without a present." He snapped open the box to reveal a small fresh-flower corsage.

She bounced on her tiptoes excitedly as he slid the corsage onto her tiny wrist. "It's roses. Look Mommy, it's my favorite."

Tess glanced up to notice the couple who appeared behind the child. They admired her new acquisition and reminded her to say thanks. Tess recognized the woman from the office photo.

She was even more beautiful in person. Somehow Tess had known she'd be delicate and exquisitely feminine. She was. With glossy red hair waving around her face, she had deep blue eyes that took Tess's measure in a glance. She smiled, a polite smile, a curious smile rather than a friendly one.

Her daughter flung herself into Anthony's arms with a heartfelt, "Oh, thank you, Uncle Anthony."

"My pleasure, little princess."

When she finally let him go, he stood and greeted her mother. "Hey, princess." He kissed her cheek. "You're here, so I guess that means you didn't have any trouble getting back."

Big princess and little princess.

"I caught the red-eye," the woman said. "No problem."

Anthony shook hands with the dark-haired man at her side then turned to her. "Tess, Harley and Mac Gerard. They're with Eastman Investigations. Harley's been in San Francisco investigating the attack."

Harley was his on-again, off-again, nonsettling ex?

Tess hadn't realized they were one and the same. That definitely said something. She wasn't sure what.

"Pleased to meet you both." She extended her hand in greeting to Harley first. "Appreciate the help."

Harley inclined her head. "If you've got a few minutes when we're done here, we'll bring you up to date."

"You found something," Anthony said, not a question.

"Hit the mother lode last night around nine."

That sounded promising, Tess thought. She also thought that compared to his wife, Mac Gerard seemed downright friendly. He welcomed her to New Orleans and thanked her for sharing in his daughter's excitement. She didn't miss the possessive arm he kept around his wife.

"It's a big day. Glad I could be a part."

Little Princess was clearly getting tired of the conversation and wanted some of the attention for herself. She stepped in front of her parents and extended her hand to Tess. "I'm Julia Antoinette Gerard. Julia for Daddy's grandma. Antoinette for my Uncle Anthony. But you can call me Toni."

"It's a pleasure to meet you, Toni. That's a very lovely name. Congratulations on starting school."

"Thank you," she said, politely. "Did you hurt your arm?"

"I broke my wrist. What do you think of my cast?" She held her arm out for inspection and hoped Toni couldn't read.

"Can I color on it, too?"

"I'd love for you to. All Uncle Anthony's brothers did, but not your Uncle Anthony. Maybe he will if you do."

Toni accepted Tess into her circle of acquaintances without another thought then pulled away to greet a long-haired woman in a gauzy dress who made her way through the crowd.

"Aunt Delilah!" she squealed. "Where's Uncle Joe?"

"Sleeping, babe. I'd have had to blast a cannon to get him out of bed before noon, but he wanted you to have this."

She whipped out a red bandanna from her purse and Toni dissolved into peals of joy. "Is it his?"

"Just like it."

Which appeared to be good enough for little Toni. Harley helped her daughter fasten the bandanna around her neck while Mac slid the camcorder off his shoulder and started taping.

Tess stood with Anthony, watching the proceedings, glad he'd brought her along today. She hadn't made sense of the whole Harley thing yet, but she liked meeting more people who so obviously cared about him. People he cared about in return.

It seemed like such a full way to live life, made her own too-busy days seem sterile and empty by comparison. Suddenly it didn't seem like such a big mystery that she'd been so bored with everything lately.

She wasn't bored now.

As Tess stood beside Anthony, she acknowledged

what she'd known instinctively from the first moment they'd met.

This man was special.

"Aunt Courtney," Toni said with another rapturous squeal. "You're here."

Courtney Gerard scooped her niece into her arms and gave a little spin. "Of course I'm here, silly. You didn't think I'd miss your first day of school, did you?"

She gazed over her niece's head in greeting then tipped her cheek for kisses from Harley and Mac. "Hey, baby bro. How are you and Mom holding up?"

"About as well as you'd expect," Harley said.

Mac gave his wife an affectionate·squeeze. "She's been second-guessing our decision to start Toni in this program."

"Nothing to second-guess. You waited the extra year." Courtney kissed her niece's cheek. "Toni's four now. A big girl all ready for an adventure."

"Agreed," Mac said. "And three hours for three mornings a week is the perfect amount of adventure."

Tess stifled a grin. Since the big girl looked raring to go, she guessed Mom was the one who couldn't handle any more. She remembered what Courtney had said at the Christmas in July event and reasoned through the connection. If Mac was Courtney's brother, then she was connected to Anthony through Harley. One more indication of how entwined their lives still were, which raised more questions that needed answers.

Courtney finally set Toni down, kissed Anthony and turned to her. "I thought I warned you about getting wrapped up with this man's family, Tess?"

"You did, but the first day of preschool is big stuff around here. Couldn't miss it."

"You got that right, but I want to know if he's brought you home for dinner yet."

Tess nodded.

"Then it's over. You'll never get away now." Courtney shook her head in feigned sympathy.

Harley watched them closely, and Tess sensed that she had just as many questions as Tess. "You've met already?"

"Tess invited our entire Big Buddies chapter to an event at the car club convention last week," Courtney explained. "It was incredible, Harley. Parade of classic cars through town. The whole park done up like the North Pole. Huge picnic. Rides. Everyone had a blast."

Tess appreciated Courtney's enthusiasm, and that she had something positive to recommend her to this woman. She might not yet understand the relationship between Anthony and Harley, but she and her family were clearly an important part of his life.

And just as she had while standing inside Mama's kitchen yesterday, Tess found herself wanting to understand who these people were. She *needed* to know if she wanted a place for herself among them.

And Tess thought she just might.

"I'm on the board of the Nostalgic Car Club—"

"Do you have an old car?" Toni asked. "Like Uncle Anthony?"

"Not quite as old as your uncle's, but mine's a very pretty purple like your dress." At least that much hadn't changed after the beating it had taken in San Francisco.

Their discussion about classic cars was cut short when the bell rang and a teacher appeared in a doorway to invite the remaining parents into the classroom. Tess couldn't help feeling for Harley as she tightened her grip on her daughter's hand and faced the teacher with suddenly misty eyes.

She wasn't the only one who noticed, either, because Mac passed off the camcorder to Anthony. "Would you do the honors?"

Anthony didn't miss a beat. He aimed the camera as Mac wrapped his arm around his wife and led his family inside.

The Aunts Courtney and Delilah followed, but Tess hung back, wanting to give them some privacy in the crowded classroom. Yet no sooner had Harley and Mac queued up to greet the teacher than Toni broke away and headed back into the hall.

She reached for Tess's hand. "I like you. Uncle Anthony looks at you like he looks at Mommy, only not sad."

Tess took the little hand, not sure what to say, so she let herself be led inside to be part of the family. And when she found herself dragged to an elementary-size table to pose for Anthony with the aunts and Toni, she felt the craziest pride to be the woman who could make this little girl's uncle smile.

ANTHONY RESISTED THE URGE to interrogate Harley and Mac in the parking lot and suggested a nearby Starbucks instead. "It's so damn hot, the patio should be empty. We can talk there."

Not only did Harley look in need of caffeine, but a distraction couldn't hurt. She'd managed a brave face while kissing the little princess goodbye, but she hadn't gotten out of the classroom door before Mac had to steer her down the hall because she was too teary eyed to see straight.

Special days were big days for moms, too.

Turned out he was right on both counts. The patio was empty, and Harley ordered a high-test brew that Mac suggested she pour over ice. Anthony wished he'd taken the suggestion. He started sweating before he'd even pulled a chair for Tess.

"The San Francisco police didn't catch the assailant who got away from you on the street," Harley told them. "And there was no tracing their vehicle."

"Stolen?" he asked.

She nodded. "Naturally. But someone posted bail like clockwork on the others, so you were right about these guys having money behind them. The judge set some pretty steep numbers so whoever sprang them not only had big bucks, but also knew how to cover his tracks."

"Seriously." Mac gave a low whistle. "I spent the last two days unraveling the money trails. *Separate* money trails. This guy didn't miss a beat."

Harley looked pleased. "But Mac did it, and we got a name."

"Who?" Tess wanted to know.

"Daryl Keene."

That clearly wasn't what Tess had expected. She sank back in her chair, obviously stunned.

"Harley thought Tess might know him," Mac said. "He's a member of the Nostalgic Car Club."

"Oh, I know him, all right."

"He's been pursuing Tess, and not taking no for an answer," Anthony explained. "I can tell you he wasn't happy when I came on the scene."

Tess scowled. "I know Daryl was annoyed when I asked you to drive the rally, possibly even angry, but enough to arrange that attack? What would be the point? I wouldn't date him before, and he can't be foolish enough to think I'd date him after what he did to you and my car."

Anthony's gaze slid to her colorful cast. Daryl might not have intended for Tess to be harmed, but he'd damn sure meant to scare her. And putting her in harm's way was just as bad in Anthony's book. Yet, he couldn't see the point, either.

"Is this guy mentally unbalanced?"

Harley shrugged. "Nothing I came across to suggest it, but what if a date with you wasn't his *only* incentive?"

Anthony knew by the gleam in those baby blues that Harley had something. "You said you hit the mother lode. What?"

"While Mac was working on the money trails, I was tracking down how your assailants got to town. They all came in on the last morning of the rally, hours before you were expected to arrive. You declared your route with the car club that morning. I talked to a guy…what was his name—"

"Ralph," Tess supplied.

"That's it. Ralph told me Daryl Keene had to fix a flat, so he didn't get on the road until a good fifteen minutes after the rest of the contestants."

Mac set his cup back on the table. "He was hanging around after everyone else had left. It's possible he could have found out what route you were driving. This Ralph told Harley he was so busy breaking down the place that he wasn't paying any attention to what Keene was doing."

"If your assailants knew your route, it couldn't have been hard to spot you. Your car's unusual."

Anthony swallowed a laugh. "No doubt about that."

"Ha, ha." Tess narrowed her gaze. "What does Daryl want?"

Harley took a long sip from her iced coffee, eyed them above the rim, clearly enjoying a chance to build the drama.

"Pleased with yourself, aren't you, princess?" he asked.

Mac rolled his eyes. "You have no idea. She killed my cell battery last night going on about how this clue panned out."

But judging by the look on Harley's face, Anthony could just guess. "You're killing me here."

Harley smiled. "Once Mac got Daryl Keene's name, I had something to run with. I wanted to track all of your assailants back to Tulsa and some connection to this guy. Seemed pretty clear-cut. But it turned out that none of these guys was from anywhere around Tulsa, so I had to do some more digging."

"And," he prompted.

"And it turns out that none of them are even from the same towns, but there is a commonality here."

"Which is?" Tess asked.

"They're all from towns where Keene Motors has a dealership."

"Really? That's interesting."

Harley nodded. "I thought so, too. So I call Mac and we start digging into these guys' finances. Not a one of them has any connection to Keene Motors, but they're all on the books in a bunch of low-end jobs that in no way account for the money they've been tossing around the past year or so. Started running searches, and you wouldn't believe what we came up with."

"Nothing too conspicuous." Mac continued. "We got

one guy's name on a furniture-delivery invoice. Made a few phone calls and found out he walked into a showroom one day and paid for twenty grand worth of furniture in cash. Another one paid off the second mortgage on his mother's house."

"Individually, none of this would raise an eyebrow," Harley said. "But when you look at it together, you've got to ask—"

"Where are these guys getting this cash?"

"Bingo," Mac said.

"So I start making some phone calls to people with law enforcement connections in these areas, and guess what I find?"

"What?" Tess asked.

"That we've got another commonality. There's been a rash of auto thefts for the past year that the police can't seem to shut down."

Mac smiled. "So Harley gets me looking into Keene's financial transactions. Remember, this guy laundered enough money to post those bonds like a pro."

"And we find out that Daryl Keene has been sending a lot of money out of the States."

"Let me guess," Anthony said. "For about a year."

Harley nodded. "The way I figure it, he's averaging about twenty stolen cars a month through his father's dealerships and pocketing about four hundred grand in profit."

Tess shifted her gaze between them. "You're kidding? Stolen cars?"

Mac shook his head. "Gets even better."

Harley smiled triumphantly, plunking her cup back on the table and leaning forward excitedly. "I don't have solid evidence yet, but I'd bet money this Daryl Keene is just the tip of the iceberg. He's been running cars through all five of his father's dealerships and sending them *out of the country.*"

"Whoa," Anthony said.

"Whoa is right," Mac agreed. "We're talking international organized crime."

"All right. I get all this about the auto thefts," Tess said. "But where do Anthony and I come in? Why would Daryl want to destroy my car and hurt him?"

"I can't prove this," Harley said. "But if Daryl Keene is raking in this kind of money off five of his father's dealerships, just think about what he could do with his foot in the door at AutoCarTex."

Anthony agreed. "Even though Keene Motors has service departments, they deal mainly in new cars. It would be a helluva lot easier to run stolen cars through a business that deals in used vehicles. AutoCarTex would look like a gold mine."

"What do you think, Tess?" Harley asked. "Any of this ringing a bell? You know this guy."

"It could explain why Daryl wouldn't take no for an answer. I always suspected something more had to be going on." She gave a soft laugh. "Figures he only wanted me to get to Daddy."

"Now how do you know that, *chère?* The man might be a thief and an idiot, but he is male."

"Are you trying to make me feel better?"

"You're oversensitive about this," Anthony said. "You think everyone wants to get to your father through you."

"They do. You included."

"Excuse me. I didn't say word one about AutoTexCare, even though I had plenty of opportunity. Didn't you notice?"

"I noticed. I figured you wanted to wait until we resolved all this, so you'd have Daddy's proper attention." She reached out to pat his hand. "I understand, Anthony. I know you worked hard pulling your proposal together. It doesn't deserve to get lost under everything that's happened."

She was serious. Sinking back in his chair, he opened his mouth then closed it again, before finally giving a snort of disgust. "Tess, that's not the reason at all. I was placing *your* safety above *my* work. I was showing you that you mean more than an introduction to your father."

Surprise flashed in those beautiful green eyes. "Oh."

"Jeez." He shook his head, not believing how she'd misinterpreted his actions. When he glanced around to find Harley and Mac watching them as if they were enjoying the show, he warned, "Don't even go there."

"Wouldn't dream of it." Harley raised her cup in salute, and Mac laughed.

Tess shook her head as if to clear it, a smile playing around her lips. "Right before the convention Daryl e-mailed me that he'd be coming to Lubbock to scout out a dealership for his daddy. I'll bet he's expanding his daddy's business since things haven't been going so well with me."

"Which might explain the attack," Anthony said, "if he wanted to undermine me with you. I wouldn't look so hot getting my ass kicked while your car got damaged and we lost the race."

"If that's what Daryl was after, then it was a stupid idea that didn't work," Tess said fiercely as she gave his hand a reassuring squeeze. "I'd bet the ranch he didn't expect you to take out six guys with guns."

There'd been only one gun and one of the guys had gotten away. But he didn't correct her, not when she seemed to enjoy defending him. Turned out he really liked the way she went all soft around the edges when she did.

He heard Harley sucking loudly on her straw, knew she was trying hard not to laugh. He didn't look at her, and asked instead, "Do you think Keene Motors is responsible for the letters Big Tex has been getting?"

Mac shrugged. "I spoke with Tess's father and had him fax copies along with the results of the handwriting analysis and the tox reports his security chief ran. I didn't see a connection, which brings us back to motive. I don't see one."

"Unless Daryl was just looking for a way to get Daddy involved," Tess said. "He's been around the car club as long as I have. He couldn't miss how Daddy gets his back up whenever I get too far out of reach. I mean, it's kind of hard to miss how protective he is."

"That's definitely a possibility." Anthony agreed. "Keene Motors brought the letters up when you asked me to drive the rally."

She nodded then looked at Harley and Mac. "So what happens now?"

"The million-dollar question," Mac said.

"We'll turn over our evidence to the San Francisco police so they can prosecute your assailants. They'll have enough to investigate Daryl Keene's involvement, too, so my guess is they'll all sing loud to get the police to cut some deals."

"Ethically, we're obligated to report our suspicions about Daryl Keene's involvement in an international auto-theft ring to the proper authorities, too," Mac explained.

"But we'll need to document our work for you, so we wanted to get the heads-up from you first."

"Any problem with that?" Anthony asked Tess.

She shook her head. "None. Do what you need to do, and thank you both for all your help. I'm so relieved to know that everything will be taken care of, and Anthony will be safe."

"I'll be safe—" He broke off when he saw her smile and realized she was teasing. "Big Tex will be pleased, too. Maybe now would be a good time to pitch my idea."

She laughed, her green eyes sparkling. Anthony glanced around the table feeling very pleased with the morning's revelations. Pleased, but not surprised, that Harley and Mac had come through for him in such a big way. And pleased by how Tess seemed to fit so perfectly into his life.

They cleared away their cups and headed to the cars together. Mac caught Anthony when he passed. "Not bad. Only two more hours to kill until we can pick up Toni from school."

"I heard that," Harley shot back.

Anthony smiled, feeling incredibly lucky today, despite bruised ribs and a smashed-up face that *still* hurt. He hoped that luck held. Now that they'd figured things out, Tess wouldn't have any reason to stay around....

Unless he could convince her she belonged here.

"SOMETHING CAME UP AT the garage so Anthony had to leave," Tess told Courtney later that day on the phone. "I offered to go along, but he insisted I stay locked inside his house with the security system on. I know you're working, but you must get off soon, or at least take a dinner break. I could hop a cab—"

"He locked you up?" Courtney asked in mock horror. "What was the man thinking? Just sit tight, Tess. I'm on my way to break you out."

"Then pick someplace good because dinner is on me."

"Hope you're hungry."

Tess was hungry, and Courtney made good on her promise. Not thirty minutes later they were being seated inside a lush French Quarter restaurant where the dinner special turned out to be shrimp étouffé.

Tess considered that a good omen.

They chatted over French coffees while awaiting their meal, and Tess explained what Mac and Harley had discovered about the car-theft ring.

"Your brother and sister-in-law are amazing," she said honestly. "I can't believe they solved this thing so quickly."

"They're quite good at what they do," Courtney agreed. "But what I find amazing is how much the proper funding and resources can accomplish. Imagine if the system could afford to put that sort of manpower on a case. It's overwhelming to think about."

There was a lot of subtext in that statement, which Tess guessed came from Courtney's experience working in the system. She volunteered as the president of the Big Buddies Society, but her day job was in social services. And Tess knew firsthand from her own work that most good causes were understaffed and underfunded, making organizations like the AutoCarTex Foundation essential for raising corporate donations.

"No argument there, but I still think a lot had to do with Mac's and Harley's skill. Not to mention how they dropped everything so the trail wouldn't get cold."

"Well, I'm glad they came through for you. But to be

honest, there never was any question. They'd be there for Anthony no matter what."

Had the opportunity not presented itself so perfectly, Tess might have squelched her curiosity, but since it had…

"Courtney, do you mind if I pick your brain a bit about your brother and Harley? I would never ask you to discuss anything you're not comfortable discussing, so just tell me to hush and I'll ask Anthony. It's just that he's been so vague I didn't want to push—"

"What do you want to know?"

Tess sipped her coffee, letting the words form in her mind before she let them out of her mouth. "Anthony told me that he and Harley dated on and off for a really long time. I'm trying to piece together what happened so I know what I'm getting myself into here. They seem really close, and everybody seems so surprised that I came back to town with him. I'm confused."

"If it's any consolation, it's not you. Confusion happens a lot around the DiLeo family."

"Yeah, I'm beginning to see that."

Courtney brushed her hair back and got straight to the point. "You're getting into something with Anthony?"

Like everyone else she'd met in Anthony's life, Courtney obviously cared a great deal, and Tess was again struck by the loyalty and love he inspired. "You know, when I met you at the convention, about the very last thought on my mind was getting involved with anyone. I had a lot of reasons—reasons that I thought were really valid—but after being with him…well, my reasons don't seem so important anymore."

Not when she had to ask if she really wanted to live her life alone? When she looked at Anthony, and all the people who loved him, it seemed clear that if she didn't let herself get involved, she'd never stop feeling restless and bored.

Tess shrugged and met Courtney's gaze. "I can't tell you what I'm getting into here. I know how I feel, but I don't know where Anthony stands. We haven't talked about anything."

"You don't know where he stands?" Courtney raised her brows, a look of such genuine amusement that Tess was suddenly sure she'd missed something obvious. "Oh, honey, you're right. We do need to talk. I'm just glad you had sense enough to call."

"Give it to me straight."

"Okay, first things first. Harley and Anthony did date. But they weren't meant to be together like *that* forever."

"They still seem to care a lot for each other."

"They do. I think they always will. He's an important part of her life, and she is of his. I can only tell you what my brother has told me, so please keep this to yourself or he'll know where you got it."

"Of course."

"Mac says it was a commitment thing. Harley and Anthony grew up together and started dating when they were young. They were busy with school and careers—doing what most people their ages do. Mac thinks they assumed their relationship would always be there. Anthony wasn't ready to commit yet, and Harley settled for what he had to offer and never pushed for more. Then my brother walked into the picture, and that was that."

"She didn't settle. She still doesn't." The memory of Anthony's explanation replayed in her memory.

"Your brother's okay with how close they are?"

"What's not to be okay with?" Courtney laughed. "You've seen Harley and my brother together. And remember they're together 24/7 between work and home. They're wild about each other, and that's only more rock solid since Toni got here. My brother knows how important Anthony is to Harley and vice versa. He respects that, and he respects Anthony."

Tess thought about the picture on Anthony's desk, the way he'd called Harley from San Francisco when he hadn't called his family. "I don't think it has always been that way for Anthony."

Courtney shook her head, looked a little sad. "I was new to the family at the time so I really can't say what was happening, but it looked pretty rough from where I was standing."

"Anthony told me it's been a long time—over five years. And in all that time he hasn't met anyone special?"

"He dates. I ran into him at a play once with a girl named…what was her name?" She smiled. "I don't remember. She was pretty, though. Long blond hair. Sweetest Prada shoes."

Tess laughed. "I'm beginning to understand why everyone was so surprised when he brought me home."

"Anthony *never* brings a date home. That's a long-standing arrangement from his Harley days. To hear his brothers tell it, he hasn't brought a woman to his new place, either."

"Oh, he didn't mention that his place was new."

Courtney shook her head. "*New* is relative. He bought that place off Mac and Harley's boss about two and a half years ago."

"What's that all about?"

Courtney shrugged. "Mama tells everyone to back off and stop making jokes. She said when Anthony finds the right girl he'll bring her home."

The *right* girl.

If Anthony hadn't brought a girl home in all this time, then what did that make her?

A crazy feeling mushroomed inside, one of those stomach-swooping feelings she hadn't felt…she hadn't ever felt. Not until Anthony DiLeo steered his shiny red muscle car across the track and stepped out with a blinding smile.

"Well," Tess said, and she barely recognized the giddy sound of her own voice. "That certainly explains why everyone has been making such a big deal about my staying at his place. I feel so much better. I was really starting to get nervous."

"About Anthony?"

"Look at him. He's drop-dead gorgeous, available, romantic, successful…. Why wouldn't he bring women home? I couldn't imagine he was gay, but I've been known to be wrong."

Courtney let out a laugh that drew attention from a nearby table. "Don't say that word around any of the DiLeo boys."

"Got it."

She smiled over the rim of her cup. "So are you getting an idea of where Anthony stands on the issue yet?"

"I think so."

And even better—she was getting a much better idea of where she stood on the issue, too.

15

ANTHONY HEARD THE CAR when it pulled up on the street in front of his place. Heading toward the door, he peered through the glass to see Tess emerging from a car he recognized—Courtney's. And she had the sense to keep driving after letting her passenger out. Tess gave a wave then headed through his front gate just as he stepped onto the portico.

Twilight cast her in shadows that bleached the color from her pretty sundress and made her seem beautiful in a surreal sort of way. The breath caught in his throat, a stunning combination of pleasure and relief.

"Couldn't you leave a note?" he asked.

She stopped, looked surprised. "I did. It's on the mantel."

He scowled, but didn't say anything. He didn't have to. That smug look on her beautiful face assured him that she knew he hadn't thought to look there.

"Were you worried about me, Anthony?"

He scowled harder.

She laughed that silvery laugh, stepped lightly up the stairs and kissed his cheek. "You were, weren't you?"

"Yes."

Okay, so he admitted it. He could have called her on her

cell, but it was sitting on the charger in his kitchen. He wouldn't have even left her at all if that important job hadn't just arrived in his garage. He'd needed to assess the damage so Sal could place orders for the parts. He'd be doing the work himself, but he didn't want Tess to know.

She breezed past him into the house. "You know, I used to get crazy when everyone worried about me. Seemed like that's all Daddy and Uncle Ray ever did. But I like when you do it. Isn't that interesting?"

What he found interesting was how she unzipped her sundress while walking into his living room. The back parted, giving him a clean shot of her creamy skin and a pink bra strap.

He flipped the lock on his door and followed, reminding himself that he was annoyed. "So what were you off doing with Courtney?"

Tess slid her dress down her arms and let it shimmy to the floor. His gaze raked up long, long legs, over her heart-shaped bottom with the pink thong strap disappearing between her cheeks, her trim waist, the matching bra strap that suddenly sprang open with an easy maneuver.

Stepping out of the circle of sundress at her feet, she went to the mantel, her strappy heeled sandals throwing her posture just enough so sleek muscles shifted with every step and her firm bottom swayed temptingly. She reached for a letter then turned to face him….

Another shrug and the pink bra slithered away and her breasts sprang free, a breathtaking display of rosy nipples and plump curves that proved he wasn't the only one being affected by this show. Not by a long shot.

"Here you go."

She handed him the letter, fingertips grazing his in a brush of warm skin. Anthony knew she expected him to open it and read the explanation for himself, but she distracted him yet again when she started rocking her hips to slip her thong panties down, down, down…

As he watched her bend over to unhook a strap from her heel, he forgot all about explanations. He would have forgotten his own name if it hadn't been embroidered on a work shirt hanging on the coatrack within eyesight.

There was no way he could concentrate in the face of this sexy assault, and he had the wild thought that if she planned to distract him like this every time he worried, he was in big trouble. This woman would run roughshod all over him, and wouldn't his brothers just love that?

That was, of course, supposing she hung around awhile, and *that* thought knocked some sense into him. He shook his head to get his brain cells working again, but when she draped herself across his leather couch, wearing nothing but her brightly colored cast and those strappy little sandals, his ability to reason went the way of his blood flow— south.

She hiked a foot over the chair arm, dangling her shoe sexily and giving him a glimpse of the goods between her thighs, all that sweet skin she'd kept cleanly shaved since Vegas…

"Go on, read my letter," she prompted.

The paper had been folded in half, a crease down the middle, his name on the front, but his fingers felt stiff as he unfolded it—all his blood had drained to his crotch.

Anthony,
Ran to dinner with Courtney to chat. Call me on
Courtney's cell if you need me. Be back soon.
Tess

Nothing earthshaking in here and he felt a little foolish.
But those few brain cells that weren't totally fixed on the
sight of her spread out on his couch—and she looked better than any fantasy calendar babe even without a car or a
timing wrench for props—locked onto a keyword. "*Chat*
about what?"

"About you."

That redirected the blood flow a bit. "What about me?"

"I wanted to know more about your relationship with
Harley."

"So you asked *Courtney?* What was the problem with
asking *me?*" He suddenly remembered his annoyance and
thought he understood the reason for her striptease.

"If you'll give me a chance to explain, I will, but you
have to come over here."

This was another trick. Tess had already dismantled his
brain with her sexy assault, and he guessed he'd be in for more
of the same if he gave in. But when she lifted her arms to him,
all that sleek skin beckoned, and he thought…what the hell?

He was living on borrowed time until he could convince
her there was a lot more in store for them than just a fling.
So far the only thing he had going for him was sex. He
wouldn't pass up a chance to get close. Especially when
she was *so* naked.

Sinking down on his knees beside the couch, he at-
tempted to hang on to his annoyance. "Let's hear it."

Slipping a hand around his neck, she idly fingered his

nape, a casual touch for touch's sake, as if she just liked touching him. "You were pretty vague when I asked about Harley before. I got the impression it wasn't easy for you to talk about her, and once I realized you'd called her and Mac for help when you hadn't even called your family, well…I wasn't sure if I should push you to tell me."

"But you wanted to know."

She nodded. "It's obvious you care a lot. I wanted to understand, so I could figure out if there's a place for me in your life."

A place in his life. He turned his face to press a kiss on her wrist, tasting the softness of her skin, not wanting her to see how much her admission meant.

They hadn't discussed anything about the future. He'd had no idea her thoughts were traveling down the same roads. Knowing who she was and how much she chafed against her father's well-intentioned smothering hadn't left him thinking he stood a chance….

"Courtney only told me that you and Harley grew up together and never got around to committing. That's all she said."

Anthony thought she sounded worried that she might have gotten Courtney into hot water, and he didn't say any differently. He was too busy figuring out what to tell her to reassure her he was over his past and more than ready to move on with his future.

The truth. That was all he had.

"Harley and I dated for so long that I honestly didn't remember a time we weren't together. We were young, so marriage was way off in the future, something we both figured would happen one day when we got around to it. But we had things to do first, school, work…you know, *living*.

I was so busy worrying about what I wanted, I wasn't paying enough attention to what I had. I just figured she'd always be there. Sure, we dated other people in between being together, but we had rules."

Tess's hand slid around his throat then down to his shirt's buttons. She loosened his collar, keeping her gaze fixed on her task, then slipped a button through a hole, then another.

He gave a laugh when she tried to shove his shirt over his shoulders one-handed, knew what she was trying to do—distract him some more.

She was succeeding. He sat up, helped her drag his shirt off.

"And…" she urged.

"And the situation with Mac came out of left field for all of us. She and Mac worked together. Had I been paying attention, I'd have realized she was in over her head. I didn't."

"That must have been hard."

He shrugged. "I knew she never meant to break the rules, no more than she'd planned to fall in love with Mac Gerard. But she did, and I loved her enough to want what was best for her. Even if it wasn't me."

"That's very honorable."

"It might sound that way, but it wasn't. Trust me. I was a total asshole."

She eyed him doubtfully.

"Not at first, maybe. I went through the motions because I knew she'd needed me, too. But afterward, I put distance between us. A lot. Even though I knew staying away hurt her. But she didn't call me on it. And I knew she wouldn't—because she felt like she'd broken the rules, too." He kissed Tess's hand, liking the feel of her warm skin, liking the way her hand felt in his. Solid. Real. "That's where the asshole part comes in. I was just vengeful enough to let her keep on thinking it."

"And she loved you enough to let you." Not a question.

He nodded. "She wanted me to make peace with the curve life had dealt us, even if it broke her heart in the process. My mother, on the other hand, didn't have nearly so much patience. She slapped me upside the head and told me to grow up. She said, I'd made my bed and now I got to sleep in it."

Tess ran her hand over his chest, a simple touch that reassured him in a way he hadn't realized he'd needed to be reassured. "At least it wasn't a knife."

He gave a laugh. "Yeah, but she didn't say anything I didn't deserve to hear. Nic, either. He gave me the mother of all lectures, but Damon...*shit*. He kicked my ass in the dojo and didn't talk to me for three months."

"Then what happened?"

"I learned to accept that life does exactly what it's supposed to, whether I agree or not. I love her, Tess. I always will. She's a part of who I am and has been for most of my life. But it's different between us now. We're in a new place, the place where we're meant to be. It might have taken me awhile, but I see that Harley couldn't have become who she is without Mac. I've made peace with that."

"Then how come you haven't brought a woman home?"

"Courtney had herself some fun at my expense tonight, hmm?"

"Don't blame Courtney. I picked her brain. I mean, let's be real, Anthony. The way your brothers keep making jokes about you bringing a girl home. If I hadn't already slept with you, I'd have thought you were gay."

He blinked.

A wicked smile curved her lips. "Well, you are pretty enough to be gay. *Usually.*"

She trailed her fingers along the healing cut on his cheek, and he caught her hand, launched himself on the couch so she couldn't get away.

"I'll give you *gay, chère.* And I'll give it to you underneath me."

Kneeing his way between her thighs, he settled on top of her so she could feel every inch of him—including the erection that wouldn't leave room for any doubts about his sexuality.

Looping her arms around his neck, she melted against him. Heat coiled inside, an urgency he'd never known, a feeling natural and right.

"For your information, I haven't brought anyone home because the women I dated were just dates. No one special. I figured I'd only get one shot at true love, and I already blew it."

"Courtney said your mother told everyone you'd bring home the right girl when you met her." She met his gaze and he could see the vulnerability behind the bravado in those beautiful green eyes. "So did you?"

"For some reason I can't begin to understand, I've been lucky enough to meet the *right* woman, the woman I'm supposed to be with."

"You think I'm the *right* woman?"

He brushed his lips across hers softly, savored the feel of her trembling in reply. "I know you are, *chère.* And I'm the *right* man for you. It's a damn good thing that I came up with my proposal or we'd have never met. But no job is worth more than what we have together. I learned that lesson the hard way. I won't take chances with you."

"Why haven't you said anything?"

He shrugged, tried to look more casual than he felt. "We haven't had enough time together. I only knew that I didn't want to let you go, and I was going to keep coming up with reasons why you shouldn't go home until I could convince you that we belong together."

She arched against him, riding his erection until he groaned aloud. "Anthony, I live in Lubbock, and have a job, too, I might add. Just because my daddy owns the company, doesn't mean I can take leave indefinitely."

His only reply was another downstroke. He might not be able to feel skin yet, but this was the next best thing.

She saw right through his game. "So what were you going to do to keep me around?"

"Hold your car hostage."

"What?" She tried to push him back so she could see his face, but he wouldn't budge, not when she felt so soft and *right* underneath him.

"You told your uncle to take care of your car repairs. I convinced him I was the only man he could trust to do the job."

"Is that where you went today?"

He nodded, feeling very pleased with himself when she nuzzled against him, obviously very pleased herself. "She was delivered safe and sound. I've already ordered parts."

"How long will repairs take?"

"Can't say. Repairing a classic is like art, *chère*. Can't rush art."

"You expect me to stay in town until you're through?"

He nodded. "I didn't think you'd want to leave your car when she's wounded."

"How bad?"

"She'll be as good as new the next time you see her."

"You won't even let me see her?"

He shook his head, nibbled the frown from her mouth with a bunch of small kisses. "She's in good hands."

Her expression visibly melted. Her arms tightened around him and she whispered, "Can we really make this happen?"

He stopped kissing and propped himself up on an elbow to stare down into her face. "We've got a few logistical problems, but I'm willing to do whatever it takes to be with you."

"I live in Texas and you live here."

"*Even* if it means I have to move to Lubbock and get a job as a mechanic in your father's service department. You'd date me if I were a mechanic, wouldn't you?"

Her fingers found his nape again, and she toyed with the hair there, drawing out the suspense, even though her wistful smile told him everything he needed to know. "You'd give up your family and friends to be with me?"

"I wouldn't exactly give them up. I just won't be around as often for Sunday dinner."

"What about your AutoTexCare plan?"

"What about it?"

"You'd give that up, too?"

"I won't take chances with you, Tess. Not for my job. Not for anything."

She slipped her legs around him, a move that spread her thighs wider, drove him a little deeper. "Daddy's going to be real disappointed, then. He thought your idea was brilliant."

"What?"

Arching her hips, she rode him a neat stroke, shivered when she caught a spot that must have felt really good.

"How would your father know about my AutoTexCare plan?"

"I told him all about it at the hospital."

Anthony exhaled heavily, wondering why he'd ever complained about being bored. Ironic how life had tossed him exactly what he'd asked for, and now he'd fallen in love with a woman who was a surprise a minute.

"So all this time when I thought I was proving I wanted you and not an introduction, I wasn't proving a damn thing?"

"You'd already proven yourself to me." There was a tenderness to her voice that told him just how serious she was. "I wasn't sure what I wanted from you, Anthony, but I knew I wasn't ready for us to be over yet."

"I got that part—you wanted to stay in San Francisco for a few extra days, remember?" Slipping a hand underneath her, he lifted her against him, another stroke that tortured him with thoughts of being inside her.

"We'd have had fun."

"We have had fun."

"Yeah. We have. I like your life. I want to be a part of it." She gave a dreamy sigh and pleasure melted over her face when she closed her eyes and let the rhythm of their rocking hips take over. "But I think you should officially present your proposal to Daddy before we try to figure out how to handle our logistical problems."

"Then I will. If he's interested, I can see a bunch of ways we might maneuver our work situations so we can be together, either here or in Lubbock."

"It'll all work out."

"Just like it's supposed to."

Anthony believed that. Tess had gotten under his skin, and when she tipped her beautiful face to his and said, "Kiss me," he could feel their future spread out before him, a promise, a challenge, the thrill of a lifetime.

Epilogue

TESS ALLOWED ANTHONY to lead her through the service center, his strong hands clamped over her eyes so she couldn't see a thing. But he led her along at a steady pace, holding her close so there was no chance she'd stumble and fall.

Having his hard body surround hers again felt so right. In the month and a half since they'd met, she'd grown familiar with the way his strong arms felt around her, the way he smelled, all freshly masculine, all Anthony. She hadn't realized when signing on to be a couple that she'd miss him so much when apart.

But she had, and that had been just one surprise as they'd spent the past month working, negotiating, arguing and making up again, while they merged their lives and careers.

She'd just arrived back in New Orleans after yet another trip to Lubbock, but this time she was here to stay.

It was the perfect solution. He owned a successful business that he wouldn't give up even though he had taken on the job of getting Daddy's service up and running with his AutoTexCare plan. She'd been wanting to spread her wings for a long time. New Orleans was far enough from Lubbock while not being too far. Daddy had his plane and his dealership here. Not to mention there were always road trips and cell phones....

After a week apart, Tess had wanted to head straight home to reacquaint herself with the man she'd lain in bed at night thinking about. Thank goodness for cell phones! When she hadn't been able to sleep in the wee hours, she'd dialed Anthony's number and they'd talked, or argued, or heated up the signal by sharing some very sexy dreams.

But right now the man wanted no part of anything except giving her a present. He'd promised to have her car completely restored as a welcome gift to her new home, and he'd apparently accomplished his goal.

When he finally brought her to a stop, she took advantage of the moment to lean back against him, to revel in the way all his hard places molded perfectly against her. He removed his hands from her face. "All right, you can open your eyes."

"First tell me—is she still purple?"

"You don't trust me, *chère?*" He sounded hurt.

"I do, but I know you think my car's ugly."

"I never said your car was ugly." He breathed the words against her ear, and she sighed aloud.

He chuckled, sending another warm blast through her, and said, "Okay."

Anthony had parked her car between the bays so it became the focal point of his big garage. On its hood was a bright red bow the size of a truck tire.

Her Gremlin was indeed still purple, its paint waxed to a highly glossed finish, all the new glass sparkling in the overhead lighting. There wasn't a trace left of the damage he'd had to pound out of her body after the tussle with the SUV. Tess would never have known the rear quarter panel wasn't brand-new.

And seeing her car and his meticulous attention to detail seemed to symbolize just how much he loved her.

"Oh, Anthony." She breathed the words on another sigh, feeling all warm and wonderful and so very pleased with life. "You do incredible work."

Shimmying close, she wrapped her arms around his neck and pulled him down so she could press appreciative kisses along his throat. She'd been waiting all week for a taste of him, wouldn't wait any longer. "I'll want to reward you, you know."

"I'm counting on it, *chère*."

"We'll have plenty of time together now."

He buried his face in her hair, inhaled deeply, leaving her no question that he'd been just as starved to see her. "I don't know about that. Corporate sent the specs for the new location. I'm looking at a lot of work to get the prototype service department up in time for construction to begin."

"As if you didn't live for challenges." And she knew that implementing his AutoTexCare plan in their new locations would be a piece of cake—especially since he was arranging for side-by-side offices in the new local showroom.

She had no doubt AutoTexCare would prove to be everything he thought it was and exactly what her daddy needed. After he got the prototypes up and running, he'd start looking at the next challenge of implementing his plan in the existing locations.

He brushed a kiss onto her hair. "So how did things work out with your staff?"

He'd known how worried she'd been. Moving the foundation out of AutoCarTex headquarters wasn't any problem since she operated independently anyway, but the others in her office…

"Found perfect positions in corporate for my office staff and it turns out that Hal wants to come here. He said New Orleans is much more along the lines of what he's used to. I didn't realize it, but he hated Lubbock and liked working for me. Coming here will solve his problem."

Anthony tightened his grip around her, pressed a kiss to the top of her head. "So everything worked out."

"Just like it was meant to."

Even the situation with Daryl was resolving itself. His thugs had done as Harley predicted and testified against him to cut their own deals. Turned out the auto-theft ring was operating out of all his father's dealerships, including the one here in New Orleans.

Eastman Investigations had been hired to assist local law enforcement in building the case, so even Harley and Mac were in on the action, which Tess thought a nice perk for their loyalty to Anthony.

Daddy had already scheduled his first trip to town at the end of the month under the pretense of checking out the new location. As construction hadn't started yet, Tess saw right through his ploy, but thought it would do him a world of good to get out of Lubbock for something other than business for a change. She was looking forward to seeing how he liked Mama DiLeo's good Italian cooking.

"So where is everyone around here?" she asked, rising up on tiptoes to look over his shoulder.

"It's Sunday, *chère.* Shop's closed."

"So there's no one here? No one at all?"

"Just you, me and your purple Gremlin."

That sounded promising. "Maybe I'll give you my reward right now."

"First you have to look inside your car."

She eyed him suspiciously. "What's more important than your reward? I'm *very* grateful, you know?"

He gave her butt a squeeze and launched her in the direction of her car. "This is."

Oh, my, my. Another surprise.

Tess couldn't imagine what he'd done inside. Naturally, she'd assumed he'd had the interior detailed since glass had been everywhere, but she could sense his excitement as he dogged her heels across the garage.

Peering inside at the pristine interior, she noticed that he'd even replaced the utility tray on the floor with an upscale model the same color as her seats. He didn't miss a trick, and again his thoroughness, knowing how much he wanted to please her, caught her in all her soft spots, and made her even more excited to please him back.

Then she caught sight of the tiny jeweler's box inside the tray. "Oh, Anthony. That's not what I think it is, is it?"

"Open it and find out."

He stepped aside so she could open the door, pleased that he'd even repaired the hinge that had made the heavy door creak. Grabbing the box, she sat down on the edge of the seat, feeling wobbly kneed in a way only this man had ever made her.

With his mouth. With his love. With his surprises. Anthony DiLeo was a thrill a minute.

He braced an arm on the roof above her and smiled down, watching her with excitement in his warm brown eyes.

She flipped open the box.

A diamond winked at her from an unusual platinum setting. Before she could make sense of what this meant, Anthony knelt in front of her, plucked away the box and removed the ring.

Reaching for her cast, he slipped the ring onto her third finger and said, "Marry me, Tess."

Their gazes met, and the tenderness she saw in his expression stole what was left of her breath. His beautiful face, the strong sculpted features, the glorious golden skin, the fading scar on his cheek, all reflected every bit of the love she felt.

"Marriage? I hadn't thought that far ahead."

"I have." He slipped his fingers through hers and gave a squeeze. "I bought my new place intending to put the past behind me. Now that I've met you, I have a future, so I want it to be our home. Not just the place you live."

The future with him suddenly swelled before her, so filled with promise that she felt tears prickle her eyes. She lifted his hand and pressed her mouth to his work-rough palm, a kiss that conveyed what no words ever could—how much she loved him.

"Yes."

He pulled her up and into his arms then, sealing the deal with a kiss that led from one thing to another and yet another.

Tess had no idea how long they stood there, wrapped in each other's arms, making out against the side of her car, but her shirt was in wild disarray and he had an erection as hard as her rear axle by the time they stopped.

"Wow," was all she could say.

He flashed that blinding grin and lifted her hand to admire his ring on her finger. "*Wow* is right."

She laughed, liking the sight, too. She'd even gotten a new cast just two weeks ago. And this one Anthony had filled with little hearts—not red, but purple.

"You're going to laugh," she said. "Or be offended. But this ring reminds me of my rims."

She positioned her hand to compare the ring to her sparkling alloy rims. "See what I'm talking about? There's something about the way these tiny diamonds shoot out from the solitaire. Am I crazy?"

He didn't reply, and she glanced around, unsure if she'd find him smiling or scowling. His bedroom eyes caressed her with a look of such promise that Tess couldn't wait for their future to begin. In bed. Soon.

"Very good, *chère*. I had this designed for you by one of Mac's friends. I brought her here to find something about your car for inspiration. She took one look at your rims, and there you have it. I wasn't sure it worked."

Laughing, Tess slipped away. She wasn't going to wait for the future and a bed. Not when she had *now* and a *hood*. She was going to perform a sexy striptease and act out one of his dreams. A well-deserved reward. "It's perfect."

And it was.

* * * * *

Look for
IN THE COLD by Jeanie London
a new suspense story
available from Signature Spotlight
in November 2005.
Also watch for Jeanie's next sexy story
appearing in a special 3-in-1 collection
coming in November 2005
in Harlequin Blaze.

**Coming in June 2005
from Silhouette Desire**

Emilie Rose's

SCANDALOUS PASSION

(Silhouette Desire #1660)

Phoebe Drew feared intimate photos
of her and her first love, Carter Jones,
would jeopardize her grandfather's
political career. So she went to Carter
for help finding them. But digging up
the past also uncovered long-hidden
passion, leaving Phoebe to wonder if
falling for Carter again would prove
to be her most scandalous decision.

*Available at your
favorite retail outlet.*